I0573885

LOST AND

FOUND

GIRLS

ELSA KURT

ELSA KURT

LOST & FOUND GIRLS

Copyright©2018 Elsa Kurt

www.elsakurt.com

Ordering Information:
Quantity sales. Special discounts are available on quantity purchases by corporations, associations, and others. For details, contact the publisher at the address above.
Orders by U.S. trade bookstores and wholesalers. Please contact authorelsakurt@gmail.com or visit www.elsakurt.com.

Printed in the United States of America

ISBN-13: 978-1-7337539-4-4

ELSA KURT

DEDICATION

To my husband, always.

ELSA KURT

CONTENTS

ACKNOWLEDGMENTS

A huge debt of gratitude goes first and foremost to my husband, Paul, whose love and support makes all things possible. Thanks to Jennifer Petrozza for being my first draft reader & consistent cheerleader. This was one of those stories that came from nowhere, or at least, that's how it seemed. I woke up one morning with the very first line in my head, "I know something you don't know," and went straight to work. A couple of months later, I had Lost & Found Girls. I love this story and hope you do as well. Now, time to work on the prequel…

LOST & FOUND GIRLS

1 SINKHOLES

"I know something you don't know."

Two girls stood at the top of a sloping embankment. One tall, one small. The grass beneath their feet was August burnt and dry. The pond that the grass met was low and still, with a sickly film of algae. Behind them, on one side, sat a tired house leaning into its cracked foundation with tired, cracked people on the inside. On the other was a smaller, tidier, but emptier home with a white picket fence. A birdhouse was staked in the center of the yard; a replica of the white dormered cape style house behind it, right down to the navy-blue shuttered windows.

"That so? You gonna tell, or am I supposed to guess?"

The pair stared disinterestedly downhill, over the rock-strewn slope at what was once a lively pond, but since had become a lazy marsh in the drought. The sun weighed heavy in the sky; the air pre-storm still and oddly quiet. Later, much later, the taller and older girl, Shayne, would think of that day only as The Day It Rained because she sometimes liked to imagine she was writing a book inside her head, giving titles to her days as though they were chapters.

She was intrigued rather than annoyed by the smaller girl's words. Mostly because she didn't say it in an obnoxious sing-song cadence; it wasn't a taunt. It was the first and likely the *only* sentence she'd speak all day. Shayne hadn't known the smaller girl very long, but she knew already she wasn't the type to play those bratty kid games. If Reyanne said she knew something Shayne didn't know, she meant it straightforward.

Shayne glanced at Reyanne—at her moppy blonde hair and faded yellow smock that hung limply over her shoulders—as she scratched her pale cheek, and then tucked her fly-aways behind her ears with nail-bitten fingers. She didn't look at Shayne, she just looked out.

Shayne followed the younger child's gaze, and even though she'd looked away from her, she knew the small-for-her-age blonde girl had begun to bite at one of those already too short nails, so she reached for her hand to distract her and tells her,

"Your mama is gonna put hot sauce on those hands if you don't quit."

Reyanne gave her a funny look, like she couldn't possibly know such a thing. But at night, with her bedroom window open to catch a warm breeze and counter the frigid air-conditioned temperature, Shayne could hear the kinds of stuff Reyanne's mama said. *Shouted.* Yes, Reyanne's mama had a loud mouth and a mean tongue, and that's exactly the kind of thing she'd say, Shayne just knew it.

Shayne's mama wasn't mean. She wasn't anything except gone; meaning the dead kind of gone, and now it was just her and papa in the quiet white house because Luke left for school not long after mama left for heaven.

She wasn't sure who missed mama more, her or papa, but she *did* know that mama's absence left a big hole in their universe. It was like that big sinkhole that opened on RT 84 a few years back, swallowed up a Buick, a mini-van, and Lester Cannon's hot dog cart; only *their* sinkhole swallowed up their words. Their *family*.

Papa was alternately angry or sad, and he was always distant. In fact, it was like Shayne wasn't even there most of the time, even when she was right behind him. In his grief, he tried to make everything that reminded him of mama disappear, as if throwing away stuff and things could erase a lifetime of memories. Although each time he did something like that, he'd go quietly in the middle of the night out to the trash bins and retrieve the boxes and bags he'd tossed in anger and bring them right back inside.

Even though Shayne knew he was 'processing his emotions' (thanks to sneaking a quick read through the *The Spouses Guide to Healing After Loss* book some well-intentioned relative left on the living room coffee table), his total disregard of her hurt. In fact, Shayne more than half thought he maybe wanted for *her* to disappear too. All on account of how much she resembled her mama.

One day, not long after mama went, papa cut her hair short. Just up and cut it. He cut it right after Aunt Coral, her mama's sister, called her 'uncanny.' Shayne wasn't quite sure what she meant by that, but it didn't sound like a compliment. She was lyin' in her bed, so tired she couldn't move, couldn't even talk for being so tired. She tried hard, but she just couldn't. Not that it mattered much, she guessed. Instead, she just retreated further into herself, drifting and floating away from the hurt.

She didn't want to believe it, but after mama died, it seemed like everyone stopped looking directly at Shayne, and if they did, it was like they were looking right through her. Even her brother, Luke. That hurt her more than anyone else. Still, she understood

Looking just like her mama as she did, it just pained everyone to look at her. Papa thought cutting her hair would fix it. But it didn't. Even if he shaved her head bald, he couldn't make her mama's hazel eyes go away, or the freckles on the bridge of her nose, and especially not the little gap between her incisor and canine on the right side. Shayne wouldn't be looking in the mirror anymore, not after papa cut all her hair off. She didn't need to see that the resemblance was still there, she could feel it.

That was the only time she cried since mama went. She cried for her long honey blonde hair, now in a trash bag by the kitchen door with banana peels and eggshells and empty cans and cartons. She cried for her mama. She cried for Luke. He may as well have been gone forever, too. College on a scholarship, across the country. He wasn't coming back. No one had to tell Shayne that, either. She just *knew*. Mostly though, right or wrong, she cried for her hair.

It must've been a catalyst of sorts. The next morning, she woke up, eyes puffy from tears, and for the first time in what felt like forever, Shayne got out of bed. She brushed her teeth and splashed cold water on her face all without looking up. She let her short hair stay however it was, unwilling to put her hands up and feel the absence. And time went on.

2 UNATTENDED

Time went on so much that six months slipped by. So much that she could feel the ends of her hair touch her shoulder if she tilted just so. Time went on even as much to put three people in the old Thompson house across the way when no one was looking. Of course, there was only Shayne and papa to look, as theirs was one of the only two houses on the dirt road makeshift street. On a Monday that empty old house's big black front door yawned out at her, and on Tuesday next it choked on the exhaust of two grown-ups and a child. *Reyanne*.

Twelve-year-old Shayne felt she was too old to be hanging around with the nine-year-old girl, but the kid was alright. Quiet as heck, but all right, nonetheless. She'd followed Shayne around like a shadow for a week before she'd come close enough to say hello. In the field, down by the pond, or near the barn, ten or twenty feet behind she'd be. Biting her nails, twirling her hair, picking at her dress, but never a word came out of her mouth.

It was the frog that got her finally. Shayne caught one by the pond. Not because *she* wanted one, but because she knew she'd get the girl to come in close for a look at it. Sure enough, the scrappy kid picked her way down the embankment, her skinny bare legs poking out from that ratty dress she seemed to always wear. When she made it about five feet away, Shayne held out the gangly frog to her, giving a head nod that said, '*C'mon, kid.*' That was The Day Shayne and Reyanne Became Friends.

Solemnly the girl approached; hands ready to accept the prize. Shayne placed the fat frog into her small hands and immediately the girl broke into a broad gap-toothed smile. It was only a moment before the frog had had enough, and with a sudden jerk and a leap, was out of her hands and back in the pond with a loud splash. The girl looked a mix of surprised, scared and dismayed, but Shayne only laughed and said,

"We didn't want him, anyhow. My name is Shayne. You're Reyanne, right? Heard your mama call your name a few times."

Reyanne nodded and looked back at her house looming over the hill, one broken and drooping shutter giving a lazy wink at the two girls below.

"You're not much of a talker, huh? That's fine by me. I like it quiet. Lets me think. You can walk with me if you want; I'm heading to the woods. There are still some wild blueberries back there. You just gotta know where to look."

From that day on, Reyanne stopped following Shayne from afar and began walking alongside her. She spoke sometimes, but only in short bursts and always to the point. The child had no fluff to her. She was odd, but in a good way, Shayne thought. She supposed that the girl's strangeness made her feel more normal. That was all she really wanted, to feel normal again.

Shayne had lots of questions for Reyanne, but she figured that a girl who *could* talk, yet *wouldn't* talk must not *want* to talk. So, she let her be, and instead listened to what she didn't say. That seemed to work just fine for little Reyanne.

For instance, that day with the frog? Shayne knew right away when that girl looked back at her house, she was worried her mean mama was looking. She didn't need her to *tell* her that. And when all those emotions went across her face after that frog leaped away, Shayne knew what that all meant, too.

The simple truth was Shayne was tired of being all alone all the time. She didn't even know she was lonely before Reyanne started following her around, but she sure knew when she *didn't* follow her. Those first two weeks in mid-summer, the girls were inseparable. Whoever woke up first on any given morning went down to the embankment and waited for the other. Neither ever went to the other's door, nor did anyone ask where they were going or what they were doing. The just wandered out and went a-walking to wherever their feet carried them. The field, the meadow, the pond, the woods. Sometimes they'd walk all the way to the gas station on Quarry Road and watch the cars come and go, but mostly they stayed away from the town, and the town stayed away from them.

They liked to pretend they were invisible. Although, when Shayne really thought deep about it, she supposed maybe they really were invisible. When *was* the last time Papa had spoken to her? She couldn't recall. Unless she counted that very morning, when he shouted,

"God-damn it, Sarah! What were you thinking?"

Shayne was so startled that she couldn't say the words stuck in her throat— *'Papa, it's me, Shayne! Don't you see, it's me?* Me, *Papa, not mama!'*

His shoulders start to shake as he gripped the edges of the kitchen sink, his back to Shayne. Papa was crying. Papa never cried. So, she ran out the door and into the woods, and ran and ran until the shaky, sick feeling in her chest went away, and she collapsed to the dirt path in a heap. It was then that she remembered Reyanne.

She'd left without a thought to her, and she was probably right at that moment sitting alone on the embankment waiting. It made her feel guilty, picturing that lonesome vision, so she pulled herself up and wound her way back to the pond. Only Reyanne wasn't there.

Shayne wasn't sure what to do. She didn't want to go home. She sure didn't want to meet Reyanne's mama or stepdad. One of Reyanne's few full sentences a few weeks back- '*Travis isn't my papa*' –was said with no more inflection or feeling than if she'd said, '*Today is Tuesday.*'

She stared up at the tired house, looking for a sign of life. Boy did she get it. The black-ish front door flung open and down the stairs went Travis, half running, half stumbling, with Reyanne's big-haired mama right behind him. She started screaming at him a string of profanities Shayne had never heard her own mama ever say. Travis ignored her, or at least tried to, as he jumped into the rusty station wagon parked alongside the house. The engine wouldn't turn over at first, and Reyanne's mama's screeches turned into cackles and caws as she pointed her long-nailed finger at him-

"Ha, haaaa! Thought you'd get outta here just like that huh, Mr. Big Shot? Where you gonna go now, you stupid old goat?"

Then the engine finally did catch, and in a cloud of dust and dry grass, Travis peeled out of the yard and onto the dusty road that led into town. As fast as before, her cackles switched to shouts of rage, then wails of anguish-

"Hey! Don't you dare leave me here alone in this place! You bastard! This God forsaken hell of a place! You come back here, damn you! Travis! Travis… please come back…"

And on she went for five full minutes, never glancing in Shayne's direction, never worrying if her daughter heard the racket. Shayne took a step toward the wailing woman, but then caught movement in the window above. It was Reyanne, looking right at Shayne. When their eyes met, she shook her head and then nodded toward the pond.

She wanted Shayne to leave her mama to her hysterics and go to the pond to wait for her. Shayne was relieved to oblige. She had no idea what to say to the woman caterwauling on her porch for the world to see.

It was a good fifteen minutes before Reyanne came skipping down the hill; gone was her awkward, unsure gait- she knew the bank as well as Shayne by then and could traipse down like a nimble Billy goat. Shayne looked at her and Reyanne shrugged. That shrug said, '*Don't worry about it, happens all the time.*'

Poor kid, Shayne thought. When *her* mama was alive, she and papa would sometimes dance slow around the kitchen some nights after dinner to the little radio on the counter. They laughed a lot, too.

Well, mama did. Papa smiled down at her as she craned her swan neck to look up at him; she breathless and flirty, he indulgent and looking love-struck. They didn't yell. Papa never left the house angry. Even when mama forgot things, and burnt dinners, or got into one of her moods, he didn't mind. He just helped her to remember, or clean up, or helped her bed. Sometimes he'd tell Luke to 'take care of it' if mama got especially clumsy or confused.

Sometimes Luke would take care of it, and sometimes he'd get mad and storm out, but quiet like so mama and papa didn't hear more than the gravel spit out from his truck tires as he left to go see his girlfriend Emma in town. When he came back, everyone seemed fine again, and that was that.

So even though their families were different, the two girls had one thing in common: they were unattended. Reyanne joked in her deadpan way once and said they were ghosts. Shayne laughed and said it sure felt that way.

Papa *did* talk to her sometimes, though. Always late at night, when he thought she was asleep. Through her bedroom door, she'd hear him,

"Baby girl? You know your papa loves you? With all my heart, I do. I'm real sorry for everything, too. It wasn't your mama's fault... it was mine. I just want you to know that. G'night now."

Shayne knew he'd be embarrassed if he knew she was awake and could hear him, so she stayed silent, content knowing that he really did still care even if he couldn't show it anymore. She wondered if Reyanne's mama ever told her she loved her.

3 RAIN

Shayne and Reyanne never quarreled, but they did sometimes disagree on where to go first. Shayne loved the pond, Reyanne loved the woods. Fortunately, they had nothing but time during that strange summer, so that was their most significant and only debate on most days. Being reasonable girls, they alternated.

On The Day It Rained, they wandered their way into the woods (after a fair amount of time at the pond) and found themselves spying on a teenaged couple from town. The pair had set down a blanket in a small clearing and was kissing so hard that Shayne thought they'd eat each other's faces off any second. Reyanne thought they were gross, and even though Shayne whispered her agreement, she secretly was fascinated.

"Tommy, stop a sec. Did you hear that?"

"Hear what, Megan? It's just some squirrels or rabbits or something. Quit bein a scaredy-cat."

"I am not scared! I'm telling you, I heard somethin'."

Shayne held her breath, hoping they wouldn't spot her and Reyanne. They were only a few yards away and barely hidden by a tree trunk. She had to keep pulling Reyanne back to keep her from walking right out in plain sight.

Just as she turned to glare at Reyanne and give her a wordless hush, Shayne heard the sound that the girl, Megan, had meant. *Tap… tap, tap… tap tap.* It was the sound of fat raindrops intermittently hitting the leafy green canopy high above their heads. A sound Rocky Hill hadn't heard in two months.

"Aw, geez, it just a little rain, is all. Don't let a little wetness stop us. Wetness…now that's what I'm talking about, you know what I me—"

"Eww, Tommy! Don't be vulgar! You gotta get me home; my father will *not* believe I was at the library if I came home all soakin' wet and covered in mud."

Tommy tried once more to persuade the pretty brunette, and when he failed to get more than a chaste peck from her pursed lips, he sighed and stood up. Still, he was a gentleman and offered his hand to the girl. She took it, and when she stood up, a full head shorter than him; she pulled him in for what Shayne supposed was a conciliatory kiss.

Shayne watched breathlessly as their heads tipped towards one another, their lips parting and then, just before their mouths pressed tightly together, she saw their tongues touch. Shayne gasped in surprise and some other feeling she couldn't name, Reyanne gave an exaggerated look of revulsion; she'd seen the kiss as well and clearly wished she'd hadn't.

Suddenly, Megan broke away from Tommy and ran, and with a laugh called behind her to the dumbstruck boy,

"Catch me if you can!"

A line even Shayne knew to be rehearsed and overused by girls acting coy. She knew as well as Tommy did that she was going to let him catch her, that it was a ploy Megan had learned from watching a movie or television show. Shayne had seen those kinds of shows, too. Whenever mama would pass out (that's what Luke called it when mama slept on the sofa), Shayne would sit quietly on the floor beside her and watch with wide eyes the soap operas and daytime movies that she'd left on. Stuff mama wouldn't allow her to watch when she was not 'passed out.' Shayne knew that this Megan girl was acting out a scene and pretending it was real life.

Then, like an afterthought, she called back,

"Oh, hey Reyanne. Nice, you brought your new friend with you! Bye, y'all!"

She was past the two younger girls in a flash and with barely a glance; Tommy quick on her heels. Neither had cared about Reyanne and Shayne's presence. It was both a relief and a disappointment. She watched them until they were out of sight, and then eyed Reyanne suspiciously. How'd she know them? Reyanne studiously ignored Shayne's questioning look. Shayne sighed, realizing there'd be no explanation given, at least not right now.

Together they walked in the opposite direction of the lovebirds, back towards home, back toward Marshall Road where only two houses stood, squared off against each other like cowboys in an old western. By the time they'd reached the woods edge, by way of the narrow path they'd worn themselves, the rain was coming down hard.

"It's rainin' cats and dogs! That's what my mama used to say."

Reyanne didn't answer, she just turned her small pointy chin skyward for a moment and let that hard rain beat on her. *Strange kid* thought Shayne. It dawned on her that Reyanne still hadn't told her the something secret that she knew, and Shayne didn't.

"Hey, so that thing you said before? That you know something I don't? How 'bout you tell me what it is. I don't feel like playing guessing games."

It seemed like the girl wasn't going to answer, so she opened her mouth to ask again, but then, ever so slowly, Reyanne turned her head to look at Shayne. There was no smile, no hint of teasing or anything. She just shrugged and said:

"You'll figure it out. Eventually."

Shayne started to speak, but Reyanne was already walking away, out from under the canopy of the trees and into the downpour. She walked purposefully, but not hurriedly even though she was soaked to the bone almost instantly. Shayne watched the slight girl trudge up the paint stripped stairs, past her mama and Travis who sat propped up against each other, brown bottles in their hands and bored expressions on their faces. Travis had returned with the beer, and it would seem their fight was forgiven and forgotten. She ignored them, and they ignored her. Her mama glanced back when the screen door creaked open, maybe to say something to her daughter, but Reyanne was already through the other side and likely halfway up the stairs to her room. After a minute they followed her in, leaving behind their beer bottles on the swayed porch steps.

Shayne was momentarily indecisive, debating whether to go home to the empty house, or back into the woods. Neither appealed to her. Back when her mama was alive, rainy summer days meant movies on the VCR and board games or puzzles. She'd make them tea with lemon and extra sugar (and special water in hers that Shayne couldn't have) and then they'd go out on the porch swing and watch the rain come down.

She was old enough now that she could make her own hot sweet tea, bring it out on the porch along with the soft thread worn blanket from the blanket chest in the foyer; maybe even a book from the bookcase mama's papa had built her way back when. But instead of giving her that warm everything-is-alright feeling, it just made her feel hollow. No, not hollow- *angry*.

Just like that: Shayne was angry. Her safe, happy life was stolen, she was robbed. She didn't know who to be angry at, though. Surely her mama couldn't have meant to leave. Papa? He was such a sad mess, lost and adrift on their dry land. Luke, well Luke just up and left them, but he had to if he ever wanted to make something of himself. It wasn't right to be mad at any of them, but here she was angry at all of them.

"It's not FAIR!"

It felt good to say the words. It felt even better to pound the wet ground with her fists.

"It's NOT FAIR!"

Shayne gulped a mouthful of air and rain, and for the first time let out the scream that she hadn't known was building up inside her. She screamed up at the sky until all the air in her lungs ran out, and her knees buckled. She screamed on that mud and a rain-soaked patch of earth at the edge of the woods until her throat hurt and her head hung in exhaustion.

She didn't know how long she stayed like that, didn't care. The relief of release was already wearing off, almost at the same rate as the rain slowed, and then stopped. The sun came back like a dimmer switch being unhurriedly raised until once again bright in the sky. She picked her head up to see the telltale end of a summer storm- a rainbow arced directly over her house.

She wanted to see that rainbow over her shingled roof as a message of good fortune and happiness, but all she saw was what it was: the diffraction of sunlight through water droplets. Pure science, as explained by her papa last year. No magic, no mystery, and no pot of gold at the end.

She started to feel foolish, sitting on the wet earth like a tantrum throwing toddler. Slowly she looked around, half expecting to see Reyanne's folks staring down at her, but there was no one. Unless she were to count the fat, silky black crow that plopped down mere feet from her knees.

He cocked his head at her, the soaking wet girl on the ground; she tipped her head at him. The crow blinked. A milky-white film slid across his jet-black eyeball, and she blinked back with cry reddened lids. Her breath slowed. His feathers puffed out. The bird surprised her again as it hopped one heavy thump toward her, craning its smooth head one way then the other to give each eye to study the sad girl.

"It's *not* fair, you know."

She startled herself by speaking aloud to the bird; he was unfazed. He hopped forward once again. He was now close enough to touch, was she brave enough to try. She wanted to, but that beak was so tar black and strong looking. She'd read once that a parrot could break your finger with its beak. Could a crow? She didn't know and wasn't about to try and find out.

The creature took a wide arced step, like a cowboy in an old western, and she marveled at how his skinny legs could hold up his comparably big body. She became aware of her own need to move, a stick or stone was digging into her shin, and once she'd noticed the discomfort, she couldn't ignore it. Risking frightening her companion, she shifted her body weight so that her legs were no longer beneath her and felt an instant rush of the pins and needles sensation flood through her legs. The bird remained.

"Well, aren't you a funny one. Not scared of nothin', huh?"

As if to show just how unafraid he was, the crow took yet another step forward, then pecked sharply at the ground several times and pointedly ignored her. Suddenly, she *wanted* to scare the night black scavenger. How dare he pay no attention to her, too? She shouted:

"HEY!"

His head again jerked up, his whole body seemed to double in size as his feathers plumped, and his beak opened wide as he let out a shockingly loud *caw* that made Shayne nearly jump out of her skin. She grabbed at the first thing her hand felt on the ground, a stumpy and gnarled stick, and drew her arm back to toss it at the beast. Before she could, he'd crouched and spread his wings, then leaped into the air with a squawk of indignation, as if she *had* thrown the stick, He was a black dot in the sky in an instant.

"Stupid bird. Stupid… *fucking* bird."

Shayne had never sworn before. She didn't know why she said that ugly exotic foreign word, but it felt good and awful at the same time. Her mama would've been appalled, papa angry, and Luke, well he'd have laughed and laughed if any of them heard her. But of course, they didn't, because Shayne was alone and not even that bold blackbird wanted to stay around her.

She recognized that she was acting dramatic—something her mama never would tolerate when she was alive, but she felt like giving herself a pity party, and so she was gonna. All she really had was little Reyanne, and that girl wasn't much. No offense to her, of course. It was probably a good thing the girl went home; Shayne felt like being mean.

Shayne was startled at that realization; her family wasn't like that. Neither mama nor papa ever raised a hand to her or Luke, ever. They were talkers, lecturers, *reason*-ers. Sure, mama would have her blue spells and black moods, but Papa always handled it- handled *her*. They didn't spank or even swear. So where did this feeling, this urge to inflict pain, come from? What if she was a bad seed and maybe that's why everyone seemed to have left her?

Just like that, the rage left her, and she was merely sad again. Deflated, hollow, empty… and still on the prickly ground and becoming painfully aware of every twig and a straw-like piece of grass poking at her hip, legs, and hand. Shayne heaved both a sigh and herself up off the ground and made the split-second decision to turn back to the woods for a walk.

4 REYANNE

Reyanne watched her new friend from the permanently filmy spire window, where she knew Shayne wouldn't notice her should she have looked up. When not with the tall girl, she was usually here, in this forgotten uppermost layer of the creaky house.

She liked the quiet of the attic; its slanted roof where the sun shone through a shingle bare spot, the boxes and trinket treasure filled trunks that, when disrupted, sent a shower of particles into the still attic air like pixie dust. Best of all was the small square space above everything else, like a sentry tower where she could pretend to be a pirate on the open sea. It could only be reached via the sharp spiral staircase that sprung up dead center of the attic floor.

When not up there, spying on the world about and below, she delighted in the mysteries and stories told from within the buckled and bowed boxes and overfilled trunks. Each box held a memory, and a history of a long life lived. Photographs and letters, ticket stubs and tax receipts, dresses, ties, and a porcelain doll; it was all the previous owners' universe packed away to either be found or forgotten. However, fortune would have it.

Reyanne was the finder of lost things. Just as she found this space and its contents, she'd found the lost girl down below in the dirt. She didn't much know what to do with either, but she did know she'd figure it out when she needed to. All she had to do was wait, and patience was indeed her virtue as fate would have it.

Three floors below were the thumps and muffled machinations of two miserable adults, her mother, and Travis. She was always thinking of things for him to do, and he was always looking for ways to please her. They surely didn't belong in that house, had no right to it, yet there they were, bold as can be. They were only going to pass through town until old Travis overheard two women in the coffee shop and relayed what he'd heard to Lena.

"I'm telling you Ruth-Ann, it's not right- alone now in that empty house on that two-house joke of a street. What was he thinking, anyhow? That he could protect her? Like none of us knew...?"

"I know, I know. But he's made it clear, Carol, he's staying there. Badgering him isn't going to make him sell and move back into town, you know. Besides, who'd buy that house? Marshall Road isn't even really a road, for God's sake. It's a dirt path that leads to two houses, and one of them's been abandoned for years now!"

"Well, it's a shame, is all. Good lookin' man shutting himself off from the world like that. Did you hear? He took a box at the post office, doesn't even get his mail delivered!"

"He's still grieving, dear. It's been just months; give him time. A loss like he's had, the burden of—why, I can't imagine."

"You know, Rick Bower, over at the Firehouse, said it was one of the worst accidents he's seen in his whole life. Oh, Ruth-Ann, every time I think of his daughter, I just…"

"Now, now. Focus on the—"

The one named Ruth-Ann paused, sensing Travis' too attentive lean in. He took his cue and paid for his coffee, leaving the two women staring at his backside in consternation as the bells above the door jangled harshly at his abrupt departure.

When he told Lena that sad story, he expected her to scoff, maybe call him a fucking sentimental moron like she usually did, but she surprised him by saying,

"Marshall Road, huh? Let's go there."

Even Reyanne's head jerked up from the back seat of the old station wagon at her mother's simple statement. It was so out of character that Travis sat slack-jawed and staring at her puffy face.

"What the HELL are you waitin' for, jackass? Let's GO, I said! Jesus H. Christ, you are some kind of ever-lovin' moron, I swear…"

She kept going, muttering and swearing under her breath, only pausing to bark out a direction intermittently,

"…God damn, fool, you are—TURN LEFT HERE—pea-sized brain—FOLLOW THE CURVE-why I ever even…"

And on she went until they pulled up on the looming, swayed house that would now be called home. Until someone came and booted them out, at least. Travis wondered how she knew to find the place but didn't dare ask a question when she was in a state. He didn't mind her temper too much, most of the time that is. He knew she couldn't help herself. That woman seen a lot of heartache in her time, and sometimes she let it out the only way she knew how: angry.

She told him once, in one of her gentler moments, that if she ever let herself feel sad, even for a second, she'd never stop. She'd cry herself to death, she said. Nope, Lena Brodowski was not goin' out like that, not if she could help it. Of course, Travis wanted to say it was no better being angry and mean all the time, but he knew better. Best not poke the bear.

Travis unloaded the car of their meager belongings while Lena stood hands on ample hips and surveyed the house and surroundings. She barely gave more than a side eye to the neighbor's house; enough to take in the picket fence, driveway, and birdhouse, then quickly look away. No cars in the drive, so that was good.

Reyanne stayed quietly in the back of the wagon, staring out the grimy window at the dilapidated house and thought it was as good a place as any these two would ever find. A broke down house for broke down people. Reyanne was only nine years old, but she could tell the road to happiness was not the one they'd all been traveling on.

The pair went around the back of the house, mercifully taking their loud voices with them, even though they still carried and echoed off the tall walls. Suddenly, and again mercifully, they dropped off as they entered through the back door. Reyanne figured it was as good a time as any to get out of the car and check out her new home.

She did a slow 180, taking in the drunken looking Victorian that seemed to lean against a mutually intoxicated willow tree, the sparsely brittle grassed yard which met an irregular line of pines that marked the start of some forest land, then an embankment that led haphazardly to a vast, oval-ish pond. She could see that beyond and around the pond spread a vast field of dead grasses and scrappy fledgling trees and a distant line of evergreens to mark the field's end. Later she'd find the remnants of a massive garden in the backyard with squash that had re-seeded itself and gone wild.

At last her eyes fell upon the only other house on the forsaken dirt road. White, like the Victorian behind her, but well-loved and tended to, quite *unlike* the Victorian. Climbing rose bushes lined the fence, draping heavily over the pickets with clusters of scarlet flowers whose heady scent carried across the way on the dry breeze.

Someone had put a lot of love into that home, that much was obvious. She took in every detail, from the birdfeeder to the dark blue shutters, and up to the second story windows. It was there that she saw the curious girl staring out at her. Reyanne was more than startled by the direct eye contact, even doubting it for a moment, until the girl raised a hand to wave, that is. Then there was no mistaking; the girl in the window was indeed looking at Reyanne.

Abruptly she turned away, fiddled with the car door handle, and then ran up the front steps of her new home. A wood framed screen door guarded the imposing looking front door behind it. Its black paint was still visible despite being deeply weather-stripped. The frame was warped, forcing both doors to gap at the top and stick at the bottom.

Reyanne had to pull twice to un-stick the screen door, shaking loose a face full of dust that would have flared her allergies were they still an issue. The second door was the opposite problem; she had to throw her body weight, slight as it was, against the wood several times. Just as it dawned on her that the door might be locked, it scraped inward, almost toppling her, with Travis at the handle.

He looked down for a moment, blinking slowly, then darted a nervous glance across the street and down the makeshift lane. They both jumped a mile when Lena bellowed from behind him,

"Quit lolly-gaggin' around and help me uncover the furniture!"

While they busied themselves flicking dingy-white sheets and years of dust off antique furniture, Reyanne toed her way up the wide staircase that ran up the center, curving its way upwards to meet a second-floor landing. A second, narrower staircase wound its way up to the attic and a spire. It was there that Reyanne would claim as her personal space, contentedly watching for her soon-to-be friend.

As if on cue, the girl came out from around the back of her house. She paused, her hands on her narrow hips, head cocked to the side as she peered at the Victorian. No doubt looking for a glimpse of the new neighbors themselves, Reyanne was certain. Was she contemplating walking across the street and knocking on the door? That would be intriguing.

Alas, the girl who reminded Reyanne of a pixie in a fairy tale shrugged her shoulders and marched toward the embankment and quickly disappeared from sight, only to reappear moments later walking past water's edge, and on towards the line of trees.

She replayed the moment from the yard over again in her mind; looking over the yard, the house, up to the second-floor window, the girl. She was certain—almost certain—that the pixie-like girl had looked directly at her. But that was unlikely, impossible even perhaps because… well, because Reyanne Brodowski was dead.

5 THE OLD MAN

Much to Shayne's dismay, The Day It Rained was the most excitement she would have for the rest of the week. The dry heat resumed right where it left off, nothing new or unusual happened, her life was just the same as it was the week before.

Still, she started each day hopefully, or at least she tried to. She got the idea from a book. In papa's study there stood three bookcases, each with eight shelves, all filled end to end and top to bottom with books. Encyclopedias, thesauruses, dictionaries, atlases, and such dominated the first. Historical and non-fiction was in the second. The third, well, the third held everything else. Papa called that bookcase 'Sarah's Smut n Stuff.' He laughed and shook his head when he said that, and mama would playfully swat his arm, telling him,

"Oh, go on now! There is no such nonsense on these shelves! Why look: Jane Austin! Emily Bronte! That right there is li-tra-ture, my dear."

"Ah, yes. I see. Funny how your Janes and Emilys don't have even a crease in their spines, but ohhh, lookie here! Your Jackie Collins and your Harlequins sure do look worn!"

He held a dog-eared tome out of reach as mama stretched and strained to knock it out of his hand, but they both laughed and laughed. She knew he was teasing just as he knew she read much more than 'smut.' Her shelves were just more diverse… and disorganized. But to Shayne, that just made them more interesting. There were cookbooks next to romance novels, classics leaning against How-To's, and biographies alongside self-help.

That's where she found *Treat Every Day Like the First Day! A Beginner's Guide to Happy Living*. Not exactly something Shayne would normally go for, but something about the woman's bouffant hair and mega-watt smile compelled her to give it a look.

The inside jacket revealed an inscription in faded blue ink:

"Sare-Bear, thought you'd get a kick out of this one. Who does it remind you of? Ha-Ha!

Bunches of love & all that crap, xo xo ~ Coral"

Mama and Coral always had 'inside jokes'-something her papa explained to mean that the two women shared a particular humor that belonged only to them. The thing Shayne noticed about their inside jokes was that it always had to do with Grandmother June (like that one most likely did) and there was always a bite and a sting to their humor that made Shayne think they weren't kidding so much.

Shayne had only met Grandmother June twice before she'd passed away and found her to be a superficially nice enough woman, yet she couldn't bring herself to like her. Of course, at four, and then at seven, she could only express those thoughts by way of blurting, '*Mama, I don't like that lady.*' However, being that she'd become a well-read young woman by the ripe old age of twelve, she was afforded a greater vocabulary and could better pinpoint the heart of her dislike.

It was this: Grandmother June was a fake; pretending to be sweet and friendly when everyone was looking, then dropping the façade when all eyes were off her. While Grandmother June's *words* were saccharine sounding, even Shayne at her youngest age could see the hard glint in her eyes, the stiffness in her pose. Plus, mama was a wreck when she came around, confirming for the intuitive young Shayne that this woman was not all she seemed. It undoubtedly was no coincidence that mama fell into one of her black moods after a visit from Grandmother June, either.

It ended up not mattering too much to Shayne; Grandmother June passed away just before her ninth birthday. Mama didn't go to the funeral, even though papa tried to convince her that *'some closure would do her good.'* All mama had to do was give him 'the look'- the one that said, *'don't try me'* and papa backed off with his hands in the air in resignation.

That night they played Yahtzee and ate homemade ice cream at the kitchen table, and no one dared mention anything about Grandmother June or funerals, even when the phone rang, and Aunt Coral's voice slurred out of the answering machine.

"Sare-Bear! Sarrrrrahhhh. I know you are right there listening to this! I know it! You bailed on me, you selfish little bitch."

Long pause, the rattling of paper, a flick of a lighter.

"You bailed, an' I'm here dealing with this shit show of a family we got. You hear me, Sarah? SHIT show."

Harsh laughter that turns into a sob.

"I shoulda did what you done. Get the hell outta Dodge, find me a man like your Paul. One that'll-that'll make me forget all the sh…"

Beeeeep went the machine. Aunt Coral had used up all the space allotted. The silence in the kitchen was deafening. Her papa's eyes were locked on mama; hers were locked on her scorecard on the table. Luke had the sense to keep his head down, wait for the moment to pass, but Shayne watched them. Papa's eyes were gentle on her mama, and her mama's eyes were threatening to spill the tears welling up. Then they cut away from the table to the cabinet where they kept the grown-up drinks, and when they did, papa's hand reached out for mama's wrist, to keep her in place, but she was too quick.

Her chair scraped against the wood floor, and in a second, she was at the refrigerator, pulling out ice cubes from the freezer and soda water from the fridge. Papa caught Shayne watching, and in an over-bright tone said,

"Alright pumpkin-pie, it's your turn!"

Obediently, she shook the blue plastic cup loudly, dumped the die onto the table, counted up her points and pretended not to notice, not to be disappointed that mama walked past them with her tall glass, ice chinking, and hips swaying as she headed towards the stairs and to her room. She left the game without a word or a glance, and they all pretended not to notice that fact for another twenty-five minutes, until finally and mercifully finishing the game and heading in three separate directions; Luke to see his Emma, papa to his office, and Shayne to her bedroom and her books.

Since then, Shayne had long exhausted every book in her own bookcase and was left to rummage through those in the office if she wanted something new to read. She wanted to ask papa to go into town with her so she could visit the library or even the bookstore, but she couldn't seem to work up the nerve. So, that meant she'd have to make do with what there was, and on that particular day in August of her twelfth year, Shayne was reading how to be happy and making a mental note that it was time to get brave and sneak one of the romance novels that were kept up high.

She struggled through almost half the book, eyes glazing and head drooping before she gave in to the fact that it was the most boring book she'd ever set eyes on. It was time for one of mama's books. Even though Papa was at work and not likely to be home for hours, she was still nervous and jumpy about going into his office, especially to steal reading material that would not be even remotely on her approved reading list, so she slipped in quickly and grabbed the first title she could reach.

Once she was out in the woods and sitting in the very same clearing that Tommy and Megan had sat in four days before, she dared to study the glossy cover. On it, a long-haired, shirtless, obscenely muscular blonde man holding the impossibly small waist of a beautiful woman in one hand, the other hand tangled up in her flowing hair as he tipped her backward. They stared into each other's eyes in what Shayne supposed to be passion, but she couldn't help but notice that the woman's position looked awkward and uncomfortable.

The raven-haired beauty was practically falling out of the top of her dress, and the bottom was hiked all the way up her thigh. She had one hand splayed on the bare chest of the muscle man, the other thrown back. Shayne couldn't tell if the woman was falling backward and he was saving her, or if she was trying to fend him off. She guessed she'd just have to read the story to find out.

Two hours later she was startled from her enrapture by a deep shadow falling over her. She looked up to see an old man staring down at her. She jumped up and away from the too close man, confused and shocked at how he could've snuck up on her so stealthily.

"Whaterya doin' in my house! Git out! Git out! I'll call the cops on ya, I will!"

Shayne's confusion deepened as her fear abated; once standing, she realized she was as tall as the old man, and he was evidently quite frail. He leaned heavily on a crooked stick; his back curved under the raggedy wool sweater that otherwise hung limply on his slight frame.

"Mister, this isn't your house. You're in the woods. Are you lost or something?"

All the old people in Shayne's family had long since died by the time she came around, except for Grandmother June, of course, and she didn't count much. Still, she knew that old people could get forgetful and confused easily. Her papa's papa had something called the Oldtimers (or something like that), and he had to be put in a home for sick old people because he kept doing crazy things like driving into town in his underwear and breaking into the neighbor's house in the middle of the night.

The old man looked around as if seeing the woods for the first time, his saggy baggy old eyes seeing the forest as if for the first time.

"But it- it was right here, I tell you. *Here*. Where'd it go? Who took my house? Who…"

He trailed off and shuffled a slow spin, seemingly forgetting the existence of the young girl who half wanted to call out some words of comfort and half wanted him to just go away again and leave her to her trashy book. She sighed, then called out,

"Hey, mister, maybe you should head on back to town? Someone's bound to be wondering where you're at, right? You, uh, know the way out? I guess I could take..."

With surprising swiftness, the old man turned back to Shayne, a joyful, relieved expression on his face.

"Idina! Is it really you? I knew you'd come back, I knew it! Come give your Teddy a hug now, don't be shy, sweetheart."

Shayne, repulsed and bewildered by his sudden shift in manner, stammered that she was not his Idina, she was just a twelve-year-old kid, but it was like he couldn't even hear her, answering aloud a voice in his own head,

"That's right, my dear! I've been waiting for you, right here, in our home. You're back now…"

Teddy drew closer and closer, and though she had plenty of time and space to run, Shayne was frozen to the spot, her back against the ridged bark of sappy pine and watching wide-eyed as the decrepit man approached. His loose neck skin quivered with each shuffle; his pale blue eyes crinkled with happiness as he moved in closer.

"That's enough, Teddy."

The small but stern voice came from behind the octogenarian; belonging to a delicate, elderly woman who, with her hands on bony hips and loose silver bun coiled on top of her head, reminded Shayne of a school teacher who'd just caught her student being naughty. She half expected her to wag an admonishing finger in his face and send him to time out.

Teddy dropped his outstretched arms down to his sides, hung his head and then did the most shocking thing yet: he laughed. Not just a chuckle, or twitter, a full-blown gut laugh that wheezed and scraped in his chest; hallmark sound of a lifelong smoker.

More confused than ever, Shayne looked from one to the other, both laughing now, although woman's laugh was subdued and accompanied by a slow head shake like one would give a precocious child.

"Aw, c'mon, Idie! Her face, it was- she was-"

Another bout of raucous laughter, this time with a knee slap for emphasis.

"Teddy, that is not funny, and you know it. Scared her half to death, you did! Time for you to shuffle along and go bother some other poor soul."

"Ah, fudge, Idina. You're no fun at all. Fine, fine, I'm a'leavin'! So long, kid. Sorry if I scared ya."

The old man sauntered past Shayne, his walking stick tucked jauntily under his arm. Gone was the shuffling gait and the aged manner, replaced by a swagger that belied his apparent advanced years. As he passed, he nodded and gave a sly wink. Shayne watched until he was out of sight, then with a question on her lips before she entirely turned to address the old woman. But she was no longer there either. She'd disappeared as quickly as she arrived. No explanation, no hello or goodbye, just POOF, here, then POOF, gone; leaving Shayne, once again, with at least a dozen questions and no answers.

She supposed if she wanted the answers to at least some of those questions, she'd have to find Reyanne, so she set off towards home, determined to go right up to Reyanne's front door if she had to.

6 LENA

"I swear to God, Travis, I swear to GOD—if you don't quit that snoring right now, I will smother you with my God damn pillow."

She meant it, too. Only for that second though. Lena knew if she killed him then she'd really be alone, and the only thing worse than being around Travis… was *not*. She didn't love him, they both knew that, but Travis always said he loved her enough for both. So, she let him love her, and gave nothing in return, unless ulcers and heartburn were something.

There were plenty of times when she thought she'd try to be a bit kinder, a little gentler, but it always came to mind when he wasn't around. The minute he came back from wherever she'd sent him to, she just felt that old familiar mean come right back into her brain again and fly right out her mouth before she could stop it.

He couldn't help his deviated septum, or his mental slowness, or his sleepy eyes any more than she could help it that genetics had made so that she came from a long line of big boned women. Good Polish stock, her father would say proudly. Back when he was proud of her. She *knew* all that, but still, he annoyed her to no end and, well, he took her abuse without question or complaint, so she kept doling it out. Sure, he straightened his backbone every once and a while and gave her a what-for. But he always came back, tail-waggin' and hopeful.

Damn fool. Damn snoring fool. She was never getting back to napping now, she figured. Heaving a heavy sigh, Lena climbed indelicately out of the creaky four poster bed. She set her wide bare feet on the stripped oak floor and heard the ghost voice of her mama in her head saying, *Get some slippies on your feet, now, Lennie before you catch your death!* It made her smile a little to think of her mama, it always did.

In fact, a lot of memories were coming back to her since they'd arrived in the little town of Rocky Hill. She supposed it had something (or everything) to do with that she was back home. About ten years too late, but home, nonetheless. Lena looked around the old familiar room—same delicate floral wallpaper, nightstands and armoire in the corner even the same four-poster bed. Didn't seem possible, but it was so.

The last letter she got from her papa was through his lawyer, some five years ago. The cancer had gone into in his brain, but not before his will had been updated. It would seem he'd had a change of heart; his cut-out daughter was now cut back *in* to the will. The house would be hers to do with as she wished. She didn't respond. At least not at first. By the time she did, he was gone from this earthly life, and she was the sole inheritor of a dilapidated Victorian with seventy-nine years of memories, furniture, and heartbreak, all collecting dust while it waited for Lennie to come back home. Oh, and a tidy sum of money in a deposit box in the local bank, she couldn't forget that, could she?

She supposed she should tell Travis that they didn't break and enter, and they weren't squatters, but she was enjoying his nervousness. Soon, she'd tell him soon. For now, though, Lena wanted to explore this grand old house, see what (if anything) had changed in all the years she'd been gone. She figured she'd start with the kitchen and work her way to her old bedroom, postponing the heartache as much and as long as possible.

Papa had bequeathed every household possession to Lena. Therefore, nothing had been touched, taken or tossed when Tadeusz Brodowski passed away in a hospice bed, alone and mercifully oblivious of the fact. He was pre-deceased by Lena's mother for more than eight years. She passed shortly after Lena left home in disgrace; a pain and guilt she relived again as she walked the quiet halls of home.

Lena didn't go to either of her parent's funerals, she couldn't. *Wouldn't.* Even when her mama died, she refused to give her papa a chance at seeing his only grandchild, despite the letters mama sent insisting she and the girl would be welcome. It was too late in Lena's mind. The damage was done, the scar too deep. *Maybe someday*, she thought, *but not yet*. Then suddenly, someday was taken away from her. Her baby girl was dead, and all that was left was her and her estranged papa, unable to fix the gaping holes in each other's hearts.

Truth was, Lena didn't want to be fixed, or whole, or better. She wanted to be angry. *Angry* was easier, it hurt less; she could make herself get out of bed, shove food in her mouth and get through the days fueled by anger. *Angry* kept people at bay; no one wanted to be around such constant hostility for long. No one except Travis, of course.

He was there when her baby girl died, though Lena didn't really know him then. He was just the shabby orderly who shuffled around the children's hospital, pushing carts with trays of bland hospital food into excessively cheery looking rooms. The bright, festive colors were meant to mask all the fear and worry of parents of sick kids in hospital beds, but it was like having clowns at a funeral. At least Lena thought so.

Travis seemed to spend an inordinate amount of time around Reyanne's area, where Lena sat day and night, trying to make small talk with Lena, offering extra pudding cups, and generally hovering. Lena was harsh with him from the get-go. She was no fool, the man had a crush on her and she had no time or interest for that nonsense. Not with her whole universe laying up in that hospital bed in a too big hospital gown on her impossibly tiny body. Leukemia. In a nine-year-old girl. What kind of God does that? Lena wanted to know; she really did. Not that she was raised religious, not by any means. But Lena needed someone or something to blame other than herself. Otherwise, she'd just kill herself from the guilt.

It didn't matter that the doctor's said no one was to blame for Reyanne's illness, sometimes it just happens. But, deep down, Lena knew it was her fault. Her sweet girl was tired and frail looking longer than she was not, but Lena kept justifying it with the fact that she'd always been on the small side, that she never was a 'run around and get dirty' kind of kid, she was a 'read books and draw pictures' kid. She had a dry sense of humor and an old soul from the moment she was born. By the time Lena realized something was wrong, it was too late. Worse yet, Reyanne had to be the one to tell her.

"Mama, I don't want you to worry, but... I'm not alright. We need- I need to see the doctor."

When she said that, it was like a curtain was pulled back and Lena could see her girl for the first time; the sallow skin, the frailness. What kind of mother doesn't see that her kid is sick? How self-absorbed and selfish she'd been, moving every few years, homeschooling her and making her miss out on having friends and just being a kid. Now it was all too late. No do-overs, no second chance. It was clear to Lena. She was being punished for her wrongdoings, and now God was taking the only thing she ever really loved, her baby girl.

For three months Lena watched her baby get poked and prodded, watched her get sicker and sicker, then briefly seem better, and then worse again. She kept hoping for a miracle, despite the doctor's grave warnings to not get her hopes up too high. Reyanne was resigned, peaceful even. She took everything that was happening to her with a grace that would seem unusual to anyone who didn't know her. But Lena knew her, and this was just like her to be so calm and accepting. It *should* have helped Lena to find some peace, knowing that a nine-year-old girl could do so with ease, yet it only made her angrier.

Lena remembered Travis from the day they came into the hospital. He was there by the check-in desk, and she had the fleeting notion that his eyes were like Paul McCartney's. He was taking in the sight of the spent little girl and her frantic mama, begging, then insisting they fix her baby, all before Lois in admitting could say,

"Good morning, how can I help you?"

Dr. Meadows, the fresh-faced young doctor who would treat Reyanne throughout her stay, was passing by at just that moment. After taking one glance at the frail child, she asked Travis to retrieve a wheelchair for the young lady. So began their whirlwind of tests and the unacceptable news of Reyanne's illness.

On that last day, when Lena walked out alone, he chased after to hand her Reyanne's favorite book, The Wind in the Willows. It was the very same one she'd walked in with months before. He followed her across the street to the coffee shop, sat down at the counter with her, and even ordered her coffee when the waitress came. Despite her abyss of shock and grief, she let Travis hover. Maybe it was *because* of her deep sorrow, she didn't know or even much care. It didn't matter at all to her whether he stayed or went; Lena

Brodowski was ready to check out of her earthly life because there was nothing left in it for her. Hell, there wasn't even a home to go to; Lena had stopped paying her rent on her side of an old duplex across town and had been sleeping in her car when not by Reyanne's side.

They drank black coffees in silence while the buzz of conversations, the clatter and clinks of spotted silverware against worn plates, and the sizzles and pops of food on the griddle rang out around them as if life just went on. They finished their second cups and being that she was one step away from being catatonic, she let Travis lead her up the street from the hospital and coffee shop to his three-room apartment on the second floor of a tenement building. She could care less what his intentions were, nothing mattered to her in those first weeks.

Turned out, all Travis wanted to do was take care of her, and she let him. She let him take care of everything, all while she laid in his narrow bed and watched his small tube television without really seeing a damn thing that was playing. She only left the small apartment once, and that was to collect her daughter's ashes from the funeral parlor.

An obscenely tan-faced man with oversized teeth and voice thick with sappy sentiment recited his *'heartfelt condolences in this time of great sorrow.'* Lena could only stare at those awful teeth and the spit on the corner of his thin lower lip. Travis had to take the urn from his outstretched hands and all but force it into Lena's. Once there, pressed against her ample bosom, she clung to it hard.

My baby. My baby. My baby. The words stuck on repeat, like a broken record in her brain and like shards of glass stabbing her heart and piercing her lungs. Travis took one look in her wild anguished eyes and nodded. Somehow, this strange little man who she knew nothing about, understood her pain. More importantly, he knew to let her be.

From there, he drove her car to the duplex she'd all but abandoned, and while she sat in the passenger seat, urn still tightly held, he knocked on the neighbor's door. After a moment Charlie, the owner of the duplex opened the door, and the men spoke for a time. She could see them nod her way, but she didn't acknowledge either, and instead stared straight ahead, even as the two men brought several boxes from the apartment and loaded them into the trunk and backseat, she just stared and stared. And when Charlie, the man who'd been her neighbor, landlord and quasi-friend for nearly three years, crouched down to speak through the partially cracked open window, she still stared blankly ahead.

The two men moved away from the car, spoke a few words before doing the awkward looking back clap and handshake thing that men do. Travis climbed back into the car and turned to say something to Lena, then thought better of it. Instead, he sighed as he started the car and turned the radio on low. Lena didn't ask what they had packed, or what they'd left behind.

At last, she slid a quick glance in his direction and with her voice rusty from disuse, rasped,

"Thank you, Travis. For everything your doin'. I don't know why you're doin' it but thank you."

Somehow, the mousy man had become something of a relief to her, and even though she'd warned him *she* had no love left to give, he stayed. For Lena, that spoke a lot more than he ever did. So: *she* stayed.

The days and weeks slipped past Lena like trees on the highway, a quick flash, and a blur and gone. She'd graduated herself to the living room and sat either on the threadbare sofa or at the rickety dinette and stared at the urn set in the middle of the table. No matter where she went in the tiny apartment, the urn was in view. She couldn't seem to pull herself away from it, from her little girl.

Travis was more than tolerant, he was accepting. When he came home from work, he'd pull two frozen dinners out from a brown paper bag, microwave them and set them on the table, and never ask once for Lena to move the urn out of the way so they could maybe talk. Eventually, Lena moved it herself, to the third-place setting.

One day, about three or four months in, Travis came home from work early, wringing his hat in his hands and blubbering. At first, Lena couldn't make out his words, then he finally, it became clear.

"Travis, are you saying you lost your job? They fired you? But why? You're a good worker, I've seen it myself!"

"They said if I left quietly, they wouldn't press charges. I couldn't even say goodbye to no one."

Press charges! Lord, what had this man done, Lena wondered. It dawned on her that she really knew nothing about him, not even how old he was. She'd been so deep in her world of pain, she hadn't cared. But now the fog was lifting, and she wanted answers.

"Travis, what did you do? Come on and tell Lena what's going on, okay?"

She realized she was speaking to him like he was a child, but damn it if he wasn't acting like one. At last, he confessed. He'd been stealing those frozen dinners from the cafeteria, along with toiletries and cleaning supplies. She sighed and looked around the dingy apartment as if seeing it for the first time. In a way, she was. This place was a dump, and she was done with it.

She was almost done with Travis, too, but one look at his pathetic face and out of some sense of guilt and gratitude, she decided to keep him.

"Travis, we're goin' on a road trip. Pack a bag."

"A-a road trip? With me? I mean, you an' me together? That sounds real nice, Lena. Where, uh, where we goin', though?"

Lena wasn't consciously sure of where they were going, at least not in that very moment, so she told Travis not to worry about that, she'd point, and he'd drive. Bless his heart, he did just as he was told.

It took all an hour to sort through the boxes he'd lugged up the stairs; she wanted very little of what was in there. A photo album, a doll, a few books and some clothes. And from the dinette table, Reyanne. Everything else was just a remnant of a life that she'd been robbed of, and she needed no reminders of that. For Travis, it was even easier; some clothes and a framed sepia photograph of a handsome couple, each with a hand on the gangly boy and a baby in the crook of the woman's arm, was all he wanted.

He loaded those meager belongings in the back of Lena's station wagon while she sat at the table, Reyanne folded in her arms. When it was time to go, they walked out the door and down the stairs without a single backward glance. She wordlessly stretched the polyester seatbelt across the urn, securing it with a firm *click*, daring Travis with her eyes to make a comment. Though Travis was not considered a man of much wit or wisdom, he knew enough to stay quiet, so he nodded his head and took his place behind the steering wheel.

Their first stop on the trip to anywhere was the bank where Travis had faithfully deposited his meager paycheck every week into a savings account for the past twenty years. He preferred to do his accounting the old-fashioned way; a dog-eared blue passbook stamped by the smiling teller (he always went to Rose, she was very nice to him). He paid his bills with money orders and his groceries with cash and never bought more than what he needed. Rose had to ask him three times if he was sure he wanted to withdraw all of his money, to which he replied, 'yes, ma'am,' each time. Turned out Travis had saved a respectable amount of money in twenty years; enough to buy a decent house and a more than a decent car if he'd wanted to. However, Travis had no interest in such things, so he just handed the oversized envelope of money to Lena when he climbed back in the wagon as if it were a bag of take-out food. Upon looking inside the envelope, Lena let out a sound akin to a hoot.

"Well, aren't you just full of surprises, Travis... wait, what's your last name?"

Travis never much cared for telling people his last name, they tended to find some humor in it, and Travis didn't understand why.

"It-it's Angel. Travis Angel. And I'd appreciate you not poking fun at me for it, thank you."

Lena stared at the man driving her car for a moment, considering.

"No, Travis, I won't make fun of that. In fact, I think it's a real nice name. Suits you just right."

Travis blushed deeply, Lena pretended not to notice, and they drove out of the city together with a companionable peacefulness, and with only one of them knowing where they were headed. It took three months, both physically and emotionally, to get back home to Rocky Hill. Every time they made some decent headway, Lena would get cold feet and order Travis to stop for a few days, picking Holiday Inns instead of run-down motels since they had the means to do so.

Rocky Hill, her hometown, was a place her family was never really much a part of. They'd farmed their own land and home-schooled their only child and went to town only as needed. Up until she was a teen, Lena loved it that way. All the way up until she resented it, then she rebelled until she got caught. Of course, it was all over a young man; spied one day while at the market.

He was tall and handsome, and he bagged their groceries, even offering to carry them out to the wagon for her and her mama. They were light and easy to carry, but Lena hushed her mama from saying so and agreed to let the man carry them out. Just before he closed the trunk, he whispered for Lena to meet him by the lake off Daley Road that night. To her own surprise, she did, and for many more nights after.

She wasn't a girl with any worldly experience, and she took his word that she wouldn't get pregnant. But she did. She couldn't wait until their next meeting to tell him, so she walked into town, heading straight for the grocery store. She spent the whole time practicing just what she'd say to him and imagining how he'd react. Only when she got there, she was met by the sight of him with his arm around a beautiful blonde. On her hip was a toddler, by her side a sullen boy.

Everything clicked into place for Lena in that frozen moment. She left without being seen and ran back home with tears of hurt and shame streaming down her cheeks. She had been played the fool by a married man. Maybe another woman would have confronted him, but Lena had a stubborn kind of pride that refused to let her do so. So now the consequence was hers to bear.

She hid her secret for as long as she could, up until the day mama came into her room, lugging a basket of fresh laundry for Lena to fold, and stopped midstride at the shock of round belly that had been hidden by loose clothing for months. Lena's shirt was raised to just below her breast, exposing a six-month sized bump that was unmistakably baby in nature.

The basket fell to the floor with a thud, Idina Longchamp's hand flew to her open mouth, and Lena hastily covered her herself up. Of course, it was too late, and neither could pretend otherwise.

"Oh, Lennie! How—I mean, who? When? I don't understand, how could this have happened. Oh, your father…"

Lena was not delicate like her mother, not in appearance or manner. No, she was her father's daughter through and through; headstrong, bold and proud, so she said what came to mind.

"Well, mama, it happened in the regular way, with a boy who no longer matters, and I'm sorry for hiding this from you, but I am not sorry for wanting this baby."

They both knew that her papa would be angry, and had he known sooner, he'd have dragged her by any means necessary to the women's clinic in Haven (certainly not to their own town clinic) and no doubt took a shotgun to that 'boy' if she'd given up his name. Still, her secret was not from fear, it was from defiance. Lena knew she couldn't ask her mama to keep silent, nor could she place the burden of telling papa on her, so she marched out to the field with mama in tow, where Papa was tending his vegetables.

What happened next transpired so quickly it seemed surreal. The sound and then the sting of papa's hand on her cheek and the taste of blood in her mouth shocked them all. He'd never, ever struck her before; it was a knee-jerk reaction to his own shock. To be so disrespected and betrayed seemed unforgivable at the moment. To Lena, his slap felt much the same.

The sounds of her mama's cries and pleading to just wait till the morning, when everyone had time to calm down, went ignored. Lena threw fistfuls of clothes and handfuls of shoes in a suitcase and swept the entire contents of her vanity into a shopping bag, all while papa sat stonily in his rocker on the porch, not rocking.

She took the key to the wagon and bolted out the door, past her papa and without saying goodbye to her mama. It was the last time she'd see either of them.

7 TRAVIS ANGEL

Travis Angel had worked in the children's hospital for all his adult life. Hired at eighteen, fired at fifty. He was a good worker, not great, but good, and he liked his job because he liked being around the children. Though he could never be called ambitious or assertive, he certainly was called kind. Or he would be, had anyone ever took the time to notice him.

Travis had mastered the art of being invisible from a young age, although for him it was of no great effort, but merely a matter of preservation. Life had thrown him a most wicked curveball, one that changed a happy eight-year old's world into one of lonely isolation and confusion. In the winter of Travis' eighth year, his universe took two distinctly sharp turns, one good followed by one very, very bad.

A shy child by nature, Travis had not many friends- none, in fact, but he had loving parents and a baby sister who he adored, so he didn't mind it very much. Three weeks before Christmas Travis received a great surprise- an invite to a birthday sleep-over party for one of his classmates. Being that there were only five boys in his girl dominated class, he suspected it was a matter of parentally forced inclusion, but he didn't mind. He was going to a sleep-over!

His parents were thrilled for him and even bought him a new sleeping bag just for the occasion. On the day of the sleep-over, he packed his own sack. After saying his goodbyes to parents and sister, he tied the sleeping bag to the back of his bike seat. Then Travis peddled happily one block over to Dylan Halston's house, where he would go on to have the best first sleep-over party ever, complete with pizza, popcorn, scary movies and chocolate chip pancakes made by Dylan's mother in the morning.

Travis was excited to go home and tell his parents all about his great time (and hug sweet little Molly, who undoubtedly had missed him), so excited, in fact, that he left his new sleeping bag behind. He burst into the house, calling out for his mother, but was met by a silent house. Strange, he thought. Could they have left for church already, without him? Usually at this time on a Sunday morning mother would be shouting from the kitchen for everyone to, *'please hurry up, we're going to be late!'* and father would stroll in laughing and teasing while Travis played with Molly on the floor.

Maybe they're upstairs, he thought. Two by two he sprung up the steps, skirting the kerosene heater at the top and guessing its presence meant that the furnace was acting up again. First, he opened the door to Molly's nursery, and upon seeing her asleep in her crib, realized that they were all likely sleeping in. Uncommon, but unsurprising with Molly's teething keeping everyone up the past several nights. Travis shrugged and gently closed her door again, and instead of going to his parent's room to see if they were awake, he decided to take advantage of the quiet house and go watch cartoons on the television in the living room.

A box of cereal tucked under his arm and his favorite blanket on his lap, the happy eight-year-old settled down in the comfy sofa to watch Scooby-Doo and Shaggy accidentally solve another mystery. That was the last thing Travis remembered of that morning, all of which he told the nurse and the social worker lady in the hospital three days later. The 'social worker lady' was named Margaret, and the case of young Travis Angel would be her last. But Travis wouldn't know that, nor would he have reason to.

Travis didn't know that Margaret—under her frizzy brown hair, thick glasses, polyester pantsuit and stern demeanor—was breaking in two over the boy's awful circumstances. Or that she hated that it was her job to tell him his life would never be the same. No, Travis only knew that this lady seemed awfully cross and was saying things that didn't make sense in his brain.

"Travis? Travis, do you know where you are? Or why you're here?"

Travis only blinked at the lady, Margaret, and at the nurse by his bed.

"Travis, you are in the Monteville Hospital, Intensive Care. You parents… and your young sister, they are- they have…"

Here Margaret stopped and looked up at the nurse. Useless thing, she was, refusing to make eye contact with Margaret in fear *she'd* have to break the news to the boy. Nine years of this thankless, Godless job and it never got easier. She never got to give the good news, the happy news. Margaret was the woman that people hated. She was the bearer of bad news. The taker of crying children from their parents. The one who nudged the same children to the front doors of strangers who would either do a terrible or a tolerable job of fostering them one, and worse—the last person they'd see before the orphanage door closed them inside.

She was done with this job. Though she didn't know it herself at that moment before telling Travis Angel that his family was all dead because of carbon monoxide poisoning, she knew it after. She went on to say to him that he was the lone survivor and would likely have permanent effects from the loss of oxygen to his brain. To herself she supposed maybe it was a mercy that his mind wasn't entirely right, perhaps he would hurt less? She didn't know.

Travis had no other family to speak of, and no one knew him enough to take him in. On the same afternoon that he was told he no longer had a family, he was transported (by Margaret) to the Monteville Home for Boys, where he would remain for ten long years, and where he learned that if you were invisible, no one would hurt you.

Margaret left Travis, that small, confused and shaky, little, lost boy in the care of people who didn't care and headed straight to her field office where she turned in her badge and quit. If she thought Martin, her supervisor, would be shocked, he was not. This job had a high burn out rate, and Margaret had lasted longer than most, to her credit. She sent Martin a single postcard two months later from Arizona, where she'd dyed and straightened her hair blonde and smooth and began introducing herself as Maggie. She tossed all her pant-suits and started wearing turquoise bangles and flowing dresses as she sold pottery from her new store. She called it 'Simply Maggie's.' Some people are fortunate that their start-over goes well, and some, like Travis, are not.

As for Travis, no one seemed to want to adopt the skinny slow boy with a sad story. It wasn't until ten years later, on his eighteenth birthday, that he was released from the care of the Monteville Home for Boys. He left with a small suitcase of his scant belongings, a job interview at the children's hospital, and an address of an apartment building one block away from the hospital. He took all things given solemnly and dutifully, and so began the second part of his life.

8 SECRETS UNTOLD

"Who said it was a secret?"

"You did, Reyanne."

"No. I said I know something you don't know."

Shayne was growing exasperated by the girl's noncommittal tone.

"So, what's the big deal? If you know something, and you want me to know it, too, then just say it."

"I can't."

"Can't or won't?"

Reyanne looked skyward for a moment, then shrugged.

"Can't."

"But it's something you want me to know?"

"Mhmm."

Summer had turned to autumn, and still, Shayne had gotten nowhere with Reyanne's secret that wasn't a secret. No matter how she asked, the little girl would not, or *could* not surrender the knowledge she held captive. It had become a game of sorts, this back and forth of questions and non-answers.

"School started three weeks ago."

"Oh?"

"Yeah. How come your mamma and Travis didn't enroll you?"

"Why are *you* not in school?"

It was a fair question; one Shayne had no answer to. There was another game of sorts that she played with her papa; one created from Hurt and called Anger. She too could give the silent treatment. No longer would she beg his attention, ask him questions, or seek his affection. She was an island apart, just as he was. So, honestly, she didn't know why she was not home-schooled, because she wouldn't ask, and he wouldn't tell. She chose not to answer Reyanne's retort.

"Anyhow, we should dress up for Halloween."

"Why?"

"I don't know, because it's fun? What do you want to be?"

"A ghost."

"Seriously, Reyanne? Bor-innng."

Again, Reyanne shrugged indifferently. Although, she wasn't entirely apathetic. She had been formulating a plan, an idea really, to help Shayne discover her truth. Since she couldn't tell her, maybe she could nudge her in the right direction.

"It'll be fun. We can include Teddy and the others, and maybe even scare our parents."

"Teddy and '*the others*'? What others? Sometimes, Reyanne, you make no sense."

As it so happened, Reyanne had gone many times into the woods without her and had met Teddy not very long after *their* first meeting, all unbeknownst to Shayne.

"You never asked if there were others," she replied blandly.

"So, if I'd asked, you'd have told me?"

"Yes." For what felt like the millionth time, Shayne blew out a gust of air from her lungs. Most deliberately, she asked, "What…others…are…there, Reyanne?"

"Um, well, there's Teddy, of course. Idina, Megan, Tommy. Oh, and Sunshine…and- no, that's it, I think. So far, at least."

"Wait. How- where… who are these people? How do you know them? Why haven't you told me about them before?"

"You didn't ask."

Shayne felt ready to explode, but instead, she remained outwardly calm. Apparently, her little friend had an entirely separate, secret life outside of Shayne, and didn't mention it… because she wasn't asked. Suddenly, a curious idea came to mind.

"Okay, so you're telling me, all I have to do is ask you a direct question, and you'll tell me the answer?"

Reyanne looked up, thinking, then said,

"Yes. I think so."

"You think so, but you don't know?"

Reyanne didn't bother answering; to her, the question was redundant, and therefore undeserving of a response again by the notion that there was something unusual- *many* things unusual about her friend. Her cryptic words, her demeanor, the way she dressed. Her jokes were dry, adult-like. The fact that she never really talked about her past, or where she came from; it all gave Shayne a sense of emotional vertigo that she was finally acknowledging to herself.

Since they'd met, Shayne had felt as though she were on the edge of a strange dream; caught between two worlds and not entirely wanting either. One was hollow, the other...*heavy*. Yes, that was it exactly; there was a lightness, an *airiness* to one side, a weight to the other, and she was walking somewhere in between the two as if trapped within a cloudy, imaginary looking glass. It kept her from asking Reyanne the question that itched the back of her brain. So instead she said,

"But, I've asked you a thousand times already."

"Wrong question."

"Then what's the right question, Reyanne? Just tell me!"

The small girl looked to be earnestly struggling to answer her. But alas, she pursed her lips together and shook her head. Instead of telling Shayne what she asked to hear, she said,

"You know the question. You just don't want to know it."

Shayne wanted to deny it, but deep down she knew it to be true. She was afraid of something; some knowledge lurking in the shadows of this dream-like state they existed in. Again, Reyanne repeated, more insistently,

"*You* know."

An expectant pause hovered between them, but Shayne instead asked,

"What kind of name is Sunshine, anyway?"

Reyanne was momentarily confused by the change in questioning but quickly recovered. With the first genuine smile Shayne had ever seen on the girl, she exclaimed,

"Oh, you must meet Sunshine! She's the sweetest dog ever. Come on!"

With an exuberance Shayne hadn't known her capable of, Reyanne leaped up and skip-ran to the woods, leaving Shayne slack-jawed and baffled as she followed in her wake. When she finally caught up, she was stopped short by the sight of Reyanne and a silky Irish Setter. The dog was wagging her fanned tail and licking joyfully at Reyanne's face, who was laughing and half-heartedly pushing the dog away.

"*This is* Sunshine! Isn't she beautiful? I never had a dog before! I was allergic."

Though still confused, Shayne couldn't help but laugh aloud and be delighted as well. She'd never had a dog either, her papa was allergic as well. The dog turned her deep brown eyed gaze inquisitively towards the sound of Shayne's laughter. Reyanne stopped laughing and looked from Shayne to the dog. Sunshine sat back on her haunches next to her human friend and whined and hedged forward; she wanted to go to see Shayne, but hesitated.

"C'mere, girl," Shayne coaxed as she kneeled.

The dog whined again, cocking her head comically. Her wet eyes scanned all around the place where Shayne knelt, and though she continued to hedge and prance her front paws into the ground, she wouldn't move from beside Reyanne.

"Is she blind, or something?" Shayne asked Reyanne.

"Or something. Come into the clearing, she'll see you better that way."

Shayne did as was told and stepped into the patch of earth that had become their hangout, and sure enough Sunshine's demeanor instantly returned to joyful exuberance as she greeted Shayne with as much glee as she had Reyanne. They played with the friendly pup for more than an hour before she gave a start as if hearing her name called from a distance. Her ears perked, and her tail froze, then wagged one quick twitch before she leaped from the clearing and dashed into the woods. Shayne felt instantly saddened by the dog's sudden departure. Reyanne took pity on her friend.

"You can see her any time you want, you know. She doesn't stay long, but she always comes if you call her."

Shayne nodded, holding back the tears that threatened to spill. She didn't want to cry in front of the younger girl. She didn't want to cry, period. Without another word, the girls stood and brushed themselves off and headed homeward. Tomorrow was a new day. But what new would it bring?

9 LIPSTICK KISSES

Halloween week arrived without fanfare from either house on Marshall Road. No jack-o-lanterns sat jauntily on porch steps, no cotton 'spider webs' clung to bushes, nor yard signs exclaiming, 'BOO!' or 'BEWARE!' It was business as usual on the two-house street. For the girls, business meant sneaking out of their houses with makeshift costumes tucked under their arms and flashlights to light their way into the woods.

Shayne was less than enthusiastic about Reyanne's plan, finding it surprisingly childish for such a typically mature girl, but she went along for lack of better ideas. She'd never had a traditional Halloween growing up, anyhow. When her mama was alive, they'd celebrated at home, just the four of them. They didn't go into town to trick-or-treat with all the other children of Rocky Hill, and since Shayne had never known different it was of no consequence to her at all. In fact, she loved their tradition.

Every year, mama and papa decorated the house inside and out; downstairs in purple, black, and orange streamers, outside with 'spider webs,' ghost cut-outs, corn stalks, and hay bales, trying to make it as festive and fun as possible for her and Luke. On the day before Halloween, they'd all go down to the furthest part of the backyard, where Papa had made a pumpkin patch, and each picks out a pumpkin to carve. Papa would pull the four pumpkins on a wagon to the front porch, and when they were finished, they stuck candles in the center to illuminate them. Yes, she *loved* their tradition.

Luke, however, did not seem to share her love. No matter how hard mama and papa tried, he sulked and gave side-eye the whole time. Even though he didn't dare complain out loud, he managed to make his displeasure well known. His problem was singular: he desperately wanted to go into town, and papa would not even entertain the conversation.

"Pop, why can't we just—"

"Luke, don't."

"But it would be just for—"

"Son, I'm not going to say it again. And you are not going to ask me again. Understood?"

"Yes, sir."

As Shayne grew older, she grew curious as well. She wondered why they didn't go into town, why they didn't *live* in town for that matter. Mama would only say things like, *Oh it's just cozier out here with our little family'* and papa would say, *Never you mind that, we have got everything we need right here.* Even Luke was mum when she asked him, giving only a shrug and a suggestion to, 'go ask them.' Ultimately, Shayne figured she'd have to find out the answer for herself, one way or the other.

Fortunately, it turned out to be easier than she would've expected and happened quite accidentally. She'd been searching for a board game in the foyer closet, but the rectangular object she pulled from a newly reachable shelf was no board game, it was a photo album. She carried the unfamiliar book to the living room and plopped down on the sofa. Shayne ran a hand across the sage green, and dusty cover, tracing the letters etched in gold script, 'Our Memories,' before opening the album to the first page. She flipped through the cellophane covered pages with confusion and surprise. On each page were pictures from another life.

It was a life where her parents and brother had existed in, but not her. There were only half a dozen pages filled in the book, the rest were blank. However, the twenty-four pictures that were pressed between the cellophane and sticky cardboard backing showed a life very different from the one they'd lived since Shayne's birth. It was a life with Paul and Sarah, the beautiful couple in front of a picket fence and a large 'SOLD!' sign beside them, but it was not the house Shayne had lived her whole life in. Another page showed a smiling Paul and Sarah, this time with baby Luke in mama's arms. Photographs of trick-or-treat costumes and buckets of candy, birthday cake candles being blown out. Christmas trees and pony rides.

The last picture was of mama and Luke, who appeared to be about six or seven. They posed beside a table with a model of the solar system, a bold 2nd place ribbon hanging from the front. Luke looked up at mama rather than the camera, unsmiling. Mama gazed into the lens in a way that could easily be mistaken as sleepily. Her coat was caught frozen in time by the click of the shutter as it slipped from her shoulder, her purse hung at the almost limp crook of her arm.

It was a look Shayne knew well on her mama's face. It was the one that turned her radiance dull, her wit to sarcasm. Usually, that look preceded messes and tears, followed by silence, closed bedroom doors, long naps and '*go on outside to play so mama can get some rest*' orders from papa. It meant mama was heading into a black spell.

Shayne touched mama's two-dimensional face, studying her in a way she never could in real life. Even disheveled, her mama was beautiful. Papa called her his 'Grace Kelly', but when he showed Shayne a picture of Miss Kelly, Shayne decided that her mama was even prettier.

"So, you finally found it, huh?"

Luke had come quietly into the living room, startling Shayne. She looked up at him guiltily, hesitating before she asked,

"You all lived in town before I was born?"

"Yup, we did. Until I was seven."

He tapped his finger on the last picture, the one with him and mama.

"We- you all moved here because of... because of mama's-"

"Because Pop wanted to protect her."

"Protect her? From what, Luke?"

Luke looked away, trying to find his response in the pattern of the curtains. With a hard set to his mouth, he said,

"From herself, I guess."

He closed the album on her lap with a soft slap of the cover and slid it off her legs and onto his own, resting his forearms on it like it'd pop open if he didn't press it down. Luke stared at the nondescript faded green cover for a moment then sighed as he stood and announced,

"Too bad it doesn't seem to be working."

They didn't speak of it again. Nor did she question papa. Certainly not mama. What would the point be? Mama's spells were as much a non-topic as was her drinking; the words '*manic-depressive*' (and later '*bi-polar*') or '*alcoholic*' were never uttered. They all pretended nothing was happening; that there wasn't this *stranger* that sometimes sat in mama's chair, wearing her clothes and smelling like her perfume, but acting alien and odd. Also, it was their normal. Shayne had never known any other way to live. It wasn't until that fateful day with the photo album, one year before mama left them forever, that she began to realize that *their* normal was maybe not everyone else's normal.

As Shayne sat remembering that day, she couldn't help but wonder *what if*. What if she *had* said something to papa? Or what if she'd confronted mama; asked her not to drink anymore? What if she could've changed the course of their whole lives just by speaking the words that needed to be spoken? Mama would've stopped drinking, maybe started taking her medicine, they could've moved back into town, and Luke could've been in school with Emma, and Shayne could've had friends.

But none of that happened, nothing had changed. But that wasn't entirely true; something had changed on that fuzzy, hard-to-remember day that mama died.

The itching sensation in her brain began again; there was something she needed to remember, but…

"Penny for your thoughts," said Reyanne, noticing that Shayne was a million miles away.

"I was just thinking… I mean, I just wonder if-"

"If you could have done something different to change things?"

"Yeah, that. I- like, not just me, all of us; Luke, my papa… mama. Why didn't any of us try at least?"

"Hmm. Well, Lena used to always say 'coulda, woulda, shoulda never gets you anywhere. No point in trying to change the past. Hey, can I ask you somethin'?"

"Sure, Rey. Go 'head."

"What do you remember about the accident?"

Shayne looked away and began fiddling with the hem of her shirt. It was a long moment before she realized that she remembered nothing, nothing at all. In fact, her last memory of her mama was of watching her get ready to go into the city for the day. Mama wanted to go to the big department store; she '*hadn't been there in ages.*' She was excited, giddy even. Shayne sat at the edge of her mama's bed as she preened before the full-length mirror in the corner of the room, mesmerized.

Sarah had donned one of her nicest dresses, Shayne's favorite. It was cream with deep blue accents, scooped low in front, exposing the swell of her breast. The smooth material hugged her waist before flaring out at her hips and ending just below her knees. She looked elegant and almost old-fashioned, like the mamas in the old black and white movies.

Shayne watched as she dabbed perfume at the base of her neck, behind each ear, and at the pulse point of her wrists. When she tried to set the bottle on the tall dresser, it toppled and fell to the floor. Some of the pale gold liquid splashed out and onto Shayne's sock, and when Sarah made no move to retrieve the bottle, Shayne picked it up for her and set it back carefully on the dresser.

When she looked back at her mama through the mirror, she could see how badly her hand shook as she applied her lipstick. Their eyes locked for a brief second and Shayne quickly looked away.

"Now, Shayne, sweetheart. This is our little secret, you hear? Our own little adventure! Now doesn't that sound perfect?"

"Uhh, yes mama. But I thought papa said-"

"Oh, never you mind what 'papa said,' silly girl!" If he didn't want us girls, to go out today, he wouldn't have left the car keys for us, would he! Now go on and get yourself ready, child. Git!"

She stood to shoo Shayne out the room, but not before placing a lipstick kiss to her forehead. That was it, her last memory of her mama- perfumed air and lipstick kisses. Everything was black after that.

"I- I wasn't with her. I was home. I don't remember even hearing about the accident."

"You sure 'bout all that?"

"What? Yes, of course, I'm sure. I mean, I'd remember if I was in an accident, Rey!"

Reyanne shrugged and backed off. It was a beginning, though. Getting Shayne to talk about the accident *had* to be a step in the right direction. In all the time they'd spent together, Reyanne could never get her to talk about that day. But instead of pressing her further she changed topics.

"Okay, so let's meet out in the clearing at say, 11:30; we can put our costumes on there. I'll have the rest of the group waiting for us. Then, right at midnight, we'll scare the heck out of our parents. Got it?"

The strangeness of Reyanne's 'plan' shook Shayne out of her troubling reverie. Suddenly, the child who *never* acted like a child... was acting like a child. A very mischievous one at that.

"So, let me get this straight: you want us to sneak out in the middle of the night, Halloween night no less, meet your weird grown-up friends in the woods, put on ghost costumes, then creep back home and stand in the middle of the street and say 'booo' and 'woooo' til our folks come out and ground us?"

Reyanne was either being obtuse, or she really didn't see the absurdity of her idea, because she merely nodded enthusiastically, pleased that Shayne remembered the plan in full.

"Great, and then what, Rey? What's the purpose of this whole thing, other than to get us in big trouble?"

"Relax, we won't get in trouble, I promise. Just… just do this for me, okay?"

Shayne sighed and shook her head- not in refusal, but defeat. *Why not*, she supposed. They certainly had nothing better to do. Besides, it was kind of funny to see the ordinarily reticent little girl acting like the child she was for once.

10 ALL HALLOWS EVE

"Travis! C'mere, will ya?" With effort, she softened her tone. "I need you to do me a favor...please. I need you to take a ride into Weathersfield for me. It's gonna take you overnight, so pack a bag."

"Uh, sure, Lena, no problem. What, uh, whatcha need me to do there?"

"I need you to take this," she said, handing him a large envelope, "and open an account in the Weathersfield First National Bank, in your name. We can always add mine later."

The envelope held six thousand dollars in cash, four less than what she'd expected to see. It was her father's secret stash of emergency money. Lena supposed her father had dug into in for one reason or another, which was no matter to her.

It came down to this: she just wanted Travis gone for a little while. She was feeling claustrophobic, even in the large house, and just didn't want him mouth breathing down the back of her neck. From the moment they had arrived she'd felt so overwhelmed with the need to be alone in the place she'd once called home, and on this day, she needed it more than ever.

"Bu-but it's Halloween."

Lena looked at Travis uncomprehendingly.

"So?"

"So, I don't know. I thought maybe-"

'You thought maybe what, Travis? That trick-or-treater would be coming by here? Oh, or that maybe we'd go trick-or-treating?"

"Wha-no, I just thought," Travis sighed, not knowing how to get the words out, "I just thought you'd be feeling sad, because, you know… kids- they love Halloween, and you must be missing, uh, be missing your little girl… more than usual that is."

He cringed and held his breath, anticipating the flurry of angry words from her mouth. Talking about Reyanne was a no go with Lena. To his surprise, she stayed silent. What Travis couldn't have known was that once there was a very different Lena than the one he knew. The Lena before Reyanne died loved Halloween; in fact, it was her favorite holiday, and not her daughter's.

Reyanne humored her mother; her elaborate costumes and decorations. One year a gypsy theme, the next pirates, then princesses, old-time movie stars, and so on. But she, little solemn Reyanne, chose the same 'costume' every year: a ghost. No matter how Lena tried to entice her with flashy, fancy outfits, she resolutely stated, *'I will be a ghost, mom.'*

If those were meant to be prophetic words, Lena had yet to see the ethereal vision of her daughter, no matter how hard she looked and listened for her. She asked and prayed for it; imagined Reyanne around every corner, on every gust of wind and creak in the floorboards. At night, she would dream of her girl, always far off in the distance, but unmistakable. She'd wake herself and Travis with her cries of, '*Reyanne!*' in the darkness.

To his credit, Travis spoke of none of this, understanding that Lena had suffered a loss that left her with an invisible gaping, cavernous wound, one that was barely covered and could be torn open with a careless word. Even still, she needed him gone. She couldn't have him following her around the big house with those puppy dog eyes, talking to her about nothing in particular just for the sake of filling the silence. No, he had to go if she were to keep her tongue and her sanity,

"Travis, please. Just do this for me, will ya?"

"Well, sure, Lena. *Of course,* I will. While I'm there, how 'bout I pick us up some seafood and cornbread, and maybe even a chocolate cake from the market for Tomorrow night?"

"Sure, Travis. That'll be nice. Why don't you go on now and get a head start? It's getting late already."

A few final instructions and reminders later, Travis was kicking up dust and gravel in the wagon, and Lena was blissfully alone. When they'd first arrived, Lena had been wary, fearful even that the ghosts of a life she'd run away from would be angry with her. She couldn't bear to be in the house alone; panicking if Travis even left her sight. Gradually, though, Lena began to welcome the memories of her mother and even her father, instead of resisting them. For the first time, she couldn't wait to be alone with her memories.

She had outgrown her need of Travis, and though she felt guilty for it, she knew it to be true. She didn't love him, she never would; it was time to let him go. The money she'd given him was his to keep, add it to his own so that he could start over. When he returned from his trip, she'd tell him as kindly as she could that it was time for him to move on. *'He'll be fine, damn it,'* she told herself. She was not going to let pity and guilt rule her decisions; this was best for both of them.

She pushed those thoughts from her mind and began walking from room to room, letting the memories flood over her. Her fingertips skimmed the old, faded wallpaper, dusty frames, and furniture as she went down the halls and into each room. Her childhood flashed before her mind's eye; vignettes of laughter and tears. Over there, in the formal living room, was where she'd fallen and cut her chin on the coffee table so deeply that her father had to stitch it closed while her mother soothed her tears. In the study, under the threadbare rug the letters L. I. L. carved jaggedly; an act of rebellion by a bored nine-year-old Lena.

Every room held a lifetime's worth of history, but none more so than her parent's favorite room, their den. Dark wood and a fieldstone framed fireplace, bookcases lined with books and their chairs set before it. His, a battered leather recliner, it's seat permanently indented. Hers, a rocking chair with a thick pad and chenille throw hung over the back. Beside hers sat a basket of colorful yarns and various knitting needles, while next to his sat a small table with a stack of newspapers.

Every night, her parents had sat together in that room after dinner. Lena was welcome, too, and sometimes she did join them, but it was the one room where she felt like an intruder. She had never thought about it back then, but standing there now, she realized how very much her parents had loved one another, loved each other's company.

Another realization set it at long last. The man who'd slapped her face that day in the garden was not the man she'd grown up respecting and loving. Long-delayed maturity made her realize it was a mistake, that reaction, and one he'd have taken back if she'd only let him. *If only she'd let him.* Lena sighed and continued her trip through time.

Time had certainly stood still for the old house, if not its inhabitants. Lena was no longer that feisty little girl, her parents were long gone. Her girl: gone. Reyanne would've adored that house, with its hiding places and long halls, its spire at the very top. *The spire*, she recalled with a gasp. Oh, how Lena had loved hiding and playing up there as a child! She'd pretended she was a pirate lost at sea, the captive princess with the long, long hair, a stow-away on a ship, an astronaut bound for space. Suddenly, she was overcome with a desire to climb the spiral stairway and revisit her favorite spot.

A flashlight in hand, she made her way up slowly, pausing only briefly at the boxes and bins brimming with the past, making a mental note to return in the daylight to rummage through them. But for now, it was on to the spire, where once upon a time the stars felt nearer and her troubles further.

She spun a slow circle in the small space. It had seemed so much bigger when she'd been smaller.

Reyanne, baby, you'd have loved it up here, she whispered. She could picture the child easily up there, her books, art papers and paints strewn around her, painting whatever she saw outside the window and tucking back her blonde hair as it fell in her face with those nail bit fingers of hers.

Lena used to get on her about biting her nails, asking, *what do you have to be nervous about, girl?* Reyanne would blink distractedly at her and shrug as she replied, *I'm not nervous, I'm distracted, and it helps me think.* Such a stupid thing to get annoyed with, Lena realized. She would let that girl bite her nails to the quick without saying a word if she could just have her back again.

Lena had been staring down out the spire window unseeingly, lost in her thoughts. She became dimly aware of a sound, sounds outside and from a distance. Was it the wind? No, the trees were still, the dirt and dust on the ground undisturbed. She strained to hear more clearly, and thought, *wolves*? Possible, she guessed. The sound grew gradually louder, closer. It wasn't wolves or wind. It was the sound of *people* trying to sound like… ghosts. *Yes*, she thought, *that's what it was*: pranksters out on Halloween night causing mischief.

Pressing her head against the cold glass, Lena scanned the street, field, and wood's edge for the sight of the hooligans, but saw nothing. The sounds were now so close that the culprits should be visible, yet still, she saw no one. Then, her peripheral vision caught sight of light from across the way. The one neighbor she had, and forgotten all about, had opened their front door and looked out into the street as well. He'd also heard the noises.

The figure, a man, leaned out from the top step of his porch, crossing his arms over his chest against the chill of the night air. He stepped back into the bright foyer and awkwardly slipped on work boots before going down the steps and into the yard. Lena's brow furrowed; there was something familiar about the man. When he stepped back into the light, she gasped.

Without thinking, she went quickly down the stairs, nearly losing her footing twice, but not stopping till at her front door. She took a deep breath and opened it.

As if being pulled by an invisible cord, Lena went down the stairs and into her yard, intent on crossing the street to meet the man face to face for the first time in over ten years. At the sight of her, he too moved toward the street, towards her.

"Lena? I don't under—is that really you?"

"Hello, Paul. Been a long time."

"Lena, I—I don't know what to say…"

"An apology might be a good start, don't you think?"

"Of course, yes. I—Jesus, Lena, this is so—I'm am sorry, so incredibly sorry. For everything. I don't expect your forgiveness. My behavior was inexcusable."

"You were a piece of shit, Paul. That's what you were. I trusted you. I thought we- well, it doesn't matter what I thought back then. It was a long time ago. But, hey, looks like your life turned out just fine, though. Good for you. Curious, though… how the hell did you end up here, across from my parent's house?"

She cut her eyes to the quaint cape with unconcealed bitterness. The 'boy' from the market had apparently continued on with his picture-perfect life and wife as if Lena had never even existed. He'd been a grown man with a wife and children, she'd been a foolish child in comparison. Falling for his charm and boyish good looks, never questioning their secrecy; she found it exciting, like a Hollywood movie script. Only he was no Carey Grant, he was just a guy escaping his staid life for a little tryst with the buxom fresh-faced beauty.

Lena had been nothing more than a distraction for him; something to make the monotonous days go by. The moment she'd seen him in the market parking lot that day so long ago, she'd realized all of that. Telling him that she was pregnant would only have hurt her further, and she was shamed enough as it was. She did the only thing that made sense to her; she ran away.

"Lena—I, yes, I was all of that and more. A lot was going on, not that I'm trying to justify, I'm not. I was a coward. I knew when you didn't meet me that night at the lake that you'd found out about... that I was married. Then, a few weeks later, I heard your mother and Janie at the market talking. She'd asked about you, and your mother said you'd moved out of town. I was a coward then, too. I should've told her... something, I don't know what, but something. If it's any consolation, Lena, my life has been anything but easy. Or happy, for that matter. Listen, come inside, let's talk, okay?"

She wanted to tell him to fuck off, drop dead. But damn it, he still held some power over her. Whatever life had supposedly done to him, his looks had suffered not at all. Sure, lines had etched their mark around his eyes, and grey hairs outnumbered the brown, but the lean and lanky frame of his younger days had now filled out to give a solid, almost squareness to his physique. So, before she could stop herself, she let him lead her across the way to his warmly lit house, the noises that had brought them out there in the first place all but forgotten.

She wanted to ask, '*won't your* wife *get mad if she finds you coziest up in the kitchen with your old fling?*' but she bit her tongue and said nothing and followed him obediently through the foyer, hallway and into his kitchen. In early years, when Reyanne was just a baby, she'd fantasize about rolling back into town, and with a baby on her hip, march back into the market to confront him in front of everyone. Or showing up at his house and meeting his wife. But her own pride and shame stopped her every time.

As time went on, she became more pragmatic and possessive of her daughter. Confronting him meant involving him, and Reyanne was all Lena had. Selfish reasons aside, Reyanne was a gift and a treasure, not someone's burden or obligation. So, she raised her girl all on her own, and as she looked around the sweet and humble home that Paul had been raising his other children in, she was hit with a rush of guilt-ridden regret. Reyanne had deserved *this* as well.

While she tried to steel herself from the rush of envy at a life she'd once dreamed of for herself, another realization struck her. There was a stillness in the house, different from a sleeping house; it felt *empty*. Puzzled, she took the seat at the scarred farmhouse style table that was offered.

Paul began busying himself with making a pot of coffee, and Lena took the opportunity to look around. The kitchen was as she'd imagined. Picture-book perfect from its lace window curtains to the pale-yellow walls. Deep blue canisters sat in a tidy row on the counter, mismatched mugs hung from hooks under the honey-colored cabinet above. Paul stood before a deep copper sink sat dead center of the long counter, washing out and refilling the coffee pot.

Self-consciously she let her eyes travel down his backside, from the cowlick in his hair, his broad shoulders, the curve of his jeans, then with deliberateness, she looked at the wide planked floor and tread wore rug under her feet at the table. It was disconcerting that he could still make her blush without even trying. Pushing that thought from her mind, she focused on a reality that she'd never contemplated: he loved his wife. She knew this as surely as she knew her own name; it was in every detail of that house. It hit her with a wave of nausea, the thought of the other woman affected, even if it was unknowingly.

"Did she know about us, Paul," asked Lena in the same moment as he asked,

"Would you like some coffee?"

"Yes," she said.

"No," he said.

Lena nodded, thinking of what to say next. Again, she looked around the room and into the adjoining living room.

"She's a very lucky—"

"She died, Lena. Eight months ago."

He turned back to the coffee abruptly and began filling their cups. Steam curled from the mugs; the coffee pot clacked loudly against the warmer as he set it back. He then set one mug before her, the other at the setting beside her. She watched him as he walked to the refrigerator, pulling out a carton of cream and waving it in her direction. She nodded yes to the cream, and he set it on the table between their mugs, along with sugar and spoons.

At last, he sat down heavily in the chair, closer to her than she'd have wished. It was surreal having him this close after so many years, he *had* to feel it as well, she thought. They both struggled for what to say next. There was so much.

Over the years Lena had convinced herself that she *hadn't* loved him; it was a young, naïve girl's folly and foolishness. He was a liar and a cheater, after all. She'd loved the *idea* of him, that was all, and nothing more. But sitting so close, glancing up at the mature version of a profile she'd studied with enamored eyes until it was memorized, smelling the familiar soap smell on his skin; it brought her back in time. It was easy to recall the young girl with her heart beating out of her chest, so full of love and adoration for this man.

She blinked hard against the images floating in her mind, *clouding* her mind and unconsciously leaned away from his closeness. If he'd noticed, he made no indication, but instead spoke with deliberation.

"If you'll allow me, I'd like to start from the beginning. I owe you a true explanation, Lena. Then, even if you still can't forgive me, you at least understand."

Lena looked away for a moment, then nodded. She would hear his story; after all this time, she would know why he did what he did, and maybe, just maybe, she would get some closure at last.

"Sarah and I met in our sophomore year of college. It was rocky, to say the least. We'd been dating for almost a year when we found out she was pregnant with our son, Luke. No one was more surprised than me, let me tell you. Sarah was... well, she had some problems, some demons that she just kinda couldn't shake. I knew she wasn't ready for a child, but she was adamant that she could handle it, and me? Well, I just loved her, and I'd have done just about whatever she wanted. I think I convinced myself that having a baby would settle her down, or something."

He paused, shaking his head for a moment, perhaps at his foolishness, then continued.

"It did, for a while, at least. She was loving, attentive, fun. She was a great mom to our boy, she really was. When we got married, we decided that she would drop out, temporarily, while I continued my studies and worked. Once Luke was a little older, and I had my degree, she could go back and finish, too. Everything was going really well, I mean, she was taking her medication, eating healthy... I thought—I thought she'd turned the corner or something."

His voice shook on the last word. Cleared his throat, took a sip of coffee and continued.

"Five years. We had five great years like that. Then Luke started school and, I don't know, it was like she became un-tethered or something. She became erratic; swore the other mothers were judging her, they hated her. I used to be able to calm her down, but this time was different. I was at my wit's end, you know? Against my better judgment, I called her estranged mother, and she offered to come out for a visit. She said she knew just how to handle Sarah's 'little problem.' I never should've let that woman come. She just made everything worse. Instead of taking her meds, she started drinking. Heavily, as I found out later. I don't know how I didn't see it, but I was so busy, I guess. Between the two jobs and helping her with Luke... I just lost track of her.

I didn't have anyone to ask for help; my folks were long gone already, her sister was a mess, and I knew her mother was no help. So, it was me, just me. Then, I remembered how great she was when Luke was born, and I got this idea; I thought, 'that's it!' She needs another baby to take care of. Sarah loved the idea, too. Before long, our little girl was here. Shayne. Spitting

image of her mother, honey blonde hair, dimples...
and such a sweet baby, easy to care for. Things seemed
okay for a while, you know?

But they weren't, not by a long shot. But I was so
busy I didn't see it until it was out of hand. I let myself
believe everything was okay, even started my own
company, landscaping. It wasn't what I'd gone to
school for, but it paid the bills pretty well. At least until
Sarah discovered the internet. She liked all the online
shopping, a lot. I didn't mind though; it made her
happy and well, it kept her home more and out of
trouble. Anyhow, it all meant we needed some extra
cash, so I went back to the market to pick up some
hours."

And here, thought Lena, is where I came in. What
a different picture than what she'd imagined. Paul took
a deep breath and exhaled slowly. He took another sip
of coffee before continuing, still not looking at Lena.

"That day you walked into the market?" He let out
a long slow whistle. "My God, Lena, you were so
beautiful. You still are. You had your long black hair

in, like, this loose braid, and when you turned to ask your mother something, it whipped me in the face. I got a big lung-full of… what was it, strawberry scented shampoo! The cashier laughed, and when you realized why, you turned pink. Even still, you looked me dead in the eye, gave me that sassy grin and said-"

"Don't stand so close to me next time." Lena finished the sentence, remembered the moment well.

"That's right. I offered to carry your bags out to your car, and when your mama started to protest, you dropped the bags into my arms and waved me along like I was your hired help. I lost my head that day, Lena. You came in like a burst of sunlight on my dark days and, well, I needed you. I craved you and that light you carried. You were saving me, and I repaid you poorly."

The memories of their brief but passionate time together flooded her brain; it was all too much. Lena took in and let out a shaky breath. To speak at that moment would be agony. All the words were pent up, under lock and long-lost key, and she wasn't prepared to break that lock, but then the words came unbidden.

"Ask me about our daughter. Ask me her name, Paul."

Paul closed his eyes tightly, pushed back from the table and pressed his palms against his lids and his elbows hard into his knees and rocked. He hadn't ever known about Reyanne, but he understood immediately. Lena had imagined this moment in many ways, all of them resulting in her feeling vindicated and avenged. This was not how she felt, though. Instead, she felt hollow and sick, but most shocking of all, she felt sorry for Paul.

"I have a child- another daughter? My God, Lena, why- how… can I meet her? Please?"

Lena made a sound somewhere between a laugh and a cry. She considered going across the street, taking Reyanne off the dining table and setting the urn before him, but at last, she said,

"She's gone, too. Seems we've both paid one hell of a price for our… indiscretion."

Paul searched her face, hoping against hope it was a vengeful and cruel joke—a retaliation for his betrayal and cowardice. *Let it be anything but true.* Her expression held no lie, only tremendous grief.

Before he could offer his useless sympathies and regrets, Lena plunged into her own story, starting from from the moment she knew she was pregnant with Reyanne, and ending with them in his wife's kitchen. She hadn't intended on telling her story. She thought she wanted to leave him empty and confused. And *yes*, she wanted him to hurt. Something else inside her begged to be told, though: her story, her truth.

They sat in silence after, both lost in separate reveries. Lena became dimly aware of a steady, soft beep somewhere in the house. It was a sound she recognized easily from her time in the children's hospital; it was the sound of a heart rate monitor. Once she noticed it, it was all she could focus on, so at last, she looked up at Paul. He had been watching her.

"Would you like to meet her? My…other daughter, Shayne."

11 THINGS THAT GO BEEP IN THE NIGHT

"Well that didn't work out as planned," announced Reyanne.

She, Shayne and their odd fellow ghosts stood center of the street, deflated and disappointed.

"Better luck next time, kiddo," said Teddy as he yanked off his sheet.

The others followed suit, all except Shayne. She was confused.

"I don't understand...they walked right by us! How could the walk RIGHT BY US and not even LOOK?"

She felt dangerously close to tears, the kind that once begun can't be stopped. The hurt was crushing, the confusion monumental. Her papa and Reyanne's mama ignored them. Oh, *and* they somehow knew each other! She stared disbelievingly at the two of them in the middle of the street, oblivious of a group of sheet wearing people around them. She watched them walk to her house together, and then turned back and looked from face to face for an explanation. Teddy and Idina looked on sadly, Tommy and Megan shared a look of pity and Reyanne… well, her expression was unreadable as she stared over at the warm glow in Shayne's kitchen window.

"Teddy," said Reyanne, ignoring Shayne's question, "is that…"

"I believe so, child. Explains a lot, now, doesn't it?"

"Why, yes, I think it does."

For Reyanne, all the puzzle pieces fell into place, and she understood why Lena chose this place to settle; it was her home. The place where she'd belonged all along, where she had amends to make and forgiveness to be found. She had brought her daughter home to be with her family. Reyanne was home now, too.

"Can someone tell me what's going on? I—"

Shayne was at her breaking point. Nothing made any sense, and it seemed like everyone else was in on some secret while she was out in the cold.

"Shayne, you're so close! You're almost ready, I think."

"Perhaps she should go inside and look for herself," suggested Idina gently.

Reyanne studied the lost girl before her, the girl she now knew to be her half-sister, and contemplated.

"Yes, I think maybe so. Shayne, all of your answers are inside that house. They have been all along, but you just weren't ready to see it. I think you're ready now, though."

Suddenly, Shayne was hesitant. The answers she thought she wanted a moment ago now scalded her senses and she jerked back. There was that elusive *something* itching again at the back of her brain; a memory, knowledge, an understanding trying to break through the dawn of realization. She didn't want to be ready. *Never mind*, she thought.

Reyanne could see her internally retreat, but could do nothing to stop her, nor could she push her forward. Just as she'd discovered *her* truths, Shayne would have to do the same. She watched her friend, her *sister*, darting her eyes from the house to the woods, deciding whether to take flight or face the unknown.

"It's okay, Shayne. Really, it is, I promise. It won't be easy, but it will be alright."

Shayne nodded her head, wanting to believe that Reyanne was right, but feared nonetheless. The others took their cues to leave the girls, and one by one gave Shayne a hug before walking off into the woods. Absently, she realized that this was the first time she'd seen any of them outside the clearing.

"Will you go with me, Reyanne?"

Together the girls walked across their street, through the open front door and sat at the kitchen table with their father and Lena. Quietly, they listened to their stories. When papa finished his, Shayne felt so sad for him, sadder than she'd ever thought possible. How he had suffered in silence as he tried to take care of everyone. He blamed and hated himself enough. Shayne could not vilify him more.

Both girls cried for Lena, her shame, heartbreak, and loneliness; Reyanne for the first time fully comprehending the depth of her mother's love. A brief wave of bitterness swept over her; she had tried so hard to reach her mother and give her some relief but failed. It wasn't fair, she raged internally. Shayne must have sensed her tension, and reached for her hand and squeezed, never taking her eyes off Paul and Lena.

It was papa she watched as they heard the words, *'ask me about our—my daughter, Paul. Ask me her name.'* Shayne gasped, then sighed her sister's name along with Lena. *Reyanne.* She turned to her for a confirmation; Reyanne nodded, and they returned their attention to their father, her mother.

All four sat in silence. A faint beep from somewhere in the house was all that could be heard. When Lena cast her eyes on Paul, Shayne felt panic rise in her chest, and when her papa said, 'would you like to meet her...', Shayne shouted,

"NO!"

As they stood to make way upstairs, she slammed her fist on the table,

"Don't, papa, please don't go upstairs!"

She ran ahead of them, pleading with them to stop.

"There's nothing to see upstairs! Nothing! Please, let's just stay down here."

With wild eyes, she begged Reyanne,

"Make them stop, Reyanne. Make them stop! I don't want to see..."

But Reyanne shook her head with a sad face and said,

"It's time, Shayne. Time to decide. Go upstairs, look, and decide."

Deflated, wary and scared, Shayne did as the younger child ordered. She followed behind Lena, who followed behind Paul, pausing only briefly to gaze into the unseeing eyes of Shayne's mama in a picture frame on the wall. Lena gave the two-dimensional woman a nod before carrying on. Shayne touched the glass where her mama's cheek was and whispered, '*I love you, mama.*'

At the door of Shayne's bedroom, they paused. Papa's hand was on the doorknob, Lena's hand tentatively on the small of his back. The girls waited with bated breath, hearing the steady beep louder from behind the door. With a gentle turn of the knob, the door pushed open, exposing a dim glow from within.

"Oh, good evening, sir! I—I wasn't expecting you to come in this late. Shall I- shall I give you some time alone?"

The night nurse, Johanna, stood from her chair in the corner, an open book falling to the floor. She was a soft looking woman with a careworn face and a graying bun at the base of her neck. She was nearing retirement; this heartbreaking family would be her last assignment before she and her husband packed up and moved to be near her own daughter and grandchildren.

Though she spoke nothing of it to the father, Johanna knew all about the terrible, tragic accident that took his wife and laid his daughter in a state somewhere between life and death, even if she came out of her coma-like state, there was no telling what her mental state would be. Based on what she learned, Johanna couldn't help but wonder if the girl was better off like this, then to have to remember what had happened.

The hospital nurses had told her the awful story; Shayne had been awake when she was flown in by air medic and told the emergency team what had happened in fits and burst of hysterics:

Her mother had been behaving erratically… *'we were going into the city to go shopping, but mama wasn't acting right.'* She tried to get her to stop the car… *'she was driving so fast and goin' over the lines.'* Then suddenly, she swerved, losing control of the car… *'we went up in the air, everything was upside down.'* They were trapped in the car... *'mama wouldn't wake up. I screamed and screamed her name, but she wouldn't wake up.'* Smoke, then fire from under the driver's side began to fill the car... *'mama, someone help my mama, please!'* Then, the haunting cries that they'd never forget... *'she's on fire! She's on FIRE! SHE'S ON FIRE!'*

Over and over that little girl screamed, so hard she burst a blood vessel in her eye before they mercifully sedated her. One of the nurses had to step outside the room, shaking and crying for the horror of what the child endured.

The medics that had been on scene had also endured her screams of terror and horror. Incredibly, the flames had barely touched her, but for singeing the ends of her hair and blackening her clothes. They managed to extradite her with perhaps seconds to spare, but not before she saw her mother consumed by fire before her very eyes, and theirs as well.

They'd done everything they could for her in the hospital, her physical injuries were mild, thanks to her seat belt, but her mind was something of another matter. She hadn't woken from sedation, despite her brain waves seeming normal. Weeks of tests showed nothing worse than some initial swelling on her brain that diminished without lasting damage. There was no explanation aside from emotional trauma.

Paul refused their recommendation of a care facility and insisted on bringing her home, opting instead for round the clock care. Johanna had been with them from their first day home, caring for the child and feeling heartbroken for the father as he stared helplessly into the room, not knowing what to do. He spoke little, but Johanna knew he harbored guilt for the accident, believing he should've prevented it. As much as she wished to console the poor man, it was not her place.

With a sense of the surreal, Shayne watched her father watch *her*, or rather her lifeless form in the hospital-style bed. Flashes of their car, fire, and the smell of burning hair and flesh filled her nostrils and she ran from the room, down the stairs. Reyanne followed her, stopping her in the kitchen just before she ran out the door into the night.

"Shayne, you can't keep running! It's time for you to remember… and decide."

"Decide? What am I supposed to decide, Reyanne?"

"You know now, you remember, don't you? You remember it all."

Shayne covered her ears, shook her head, and tried to stop the flood of images, but they kept pounding at her from every direction. The whoosh of air as the car flipped, the Police on the radio singing 'every little thing she do is magic', then the metallic crack and squeal of metal against concrete, sparks flying, as they slid and scraped to a stop against a barrier. Then: silence, a deafening quiet, then a hiss from somewhere outside the car. Shayne's breath fats and heavy as the weight and pressure of her own body constricted her airway. The world was upside down. Then: smoke. Fire. Screams so wretched coming from... someone. Who, who was screaming like that, she dimly wondered? She wanted to cover her ears, her eyes, her face, anything to stop what she was seeing, hearing and smelling.

The flames climbed up her mother's legs, a trickle of blood trailed from the corner of her perfect mouth, more from her ear. Her mama's eyes were wide open, but she wasn't blinking. She just stared past Shayne. She wanted to tell her mama to stop screaming, they'd be okay, but mama wasn't the one screaming. It was Shayne, the part of her that knew her mama was dead, and the fire was eating her up, and there was no way out.

"Mama, please, please! Get us out of here! Mama! MAMA!"

Still, the flames climbed, lazy and flicking like snakes until they caught the hem of her beautiful dress, then they went wild. Shayne screamed louder, recoiling from the flames as much as the vision.

Shayne remembered everything.

The passenger door was suddenly yanked open, more metallic scrapes, and male voices shouted, *'you're okay, darlin', you're okay! We've got you now.'* The sky, impossibly blue and clear. A red-faced man, sweat pouring down his temples and looking like he wanted to cry, too as he carried her to the stretcher. He and other tied her down and braced her neck, all the while, she screamed, *'get my mama! She's on fire! Get my mama!'* Then there was the loud whine of the helicopter engine and the 'whoop, whoop' of the blades, the ear popping change in altitude, She frantically talked over all of it, over the shouts of vital signs, the questions, the air rushing all around them.

The last memory was of the sharp sting of a needle and a warm rush of calm as she drifted off and mercifully away from it all. With a gasp, she dropped her hands from her head. *She remembered everything.* Shayne sank to the floor, burying her head in her hands. Reyanne knelt beside her, close, but not touching.

"You can- you can stay with us, Shayne. With me, and Teddy and Idina, Tommy and Megan. And Sunshine, too, Or…"

'Or I can go back? To Papa and Luke?"

"Yes, but you must decide, Shayne. It's time."

"It hurts, Rey. It hurts so much to remember. If I stay, will I forget again?"

Reyanne shrugged. She honestly didn't know. However, she *did* know what Shayne would decide.

"You're going back, aren't you?"

Reyanne knew it the moment Shayne heard her papa's voice; she was choosing life over death. And at that moment, Shayne's form began to waver, like a mirage in the desert. She was in both places at once, just as she'd been for all those months, but now she knew it, too.

"I- I think I am, Rey. I'm sorry."

Reyanne shrugged and smiled her knowing smile.

"It's okay, Shayne. It's what's meant to be. I'm glad we met; it was nice having a sister, even for just a little while."

"Will I forget you, you think?"

"Not really sure. But… if you do remember, will you tell my mother something for me?"

12 DECISIONS

"The doctors say there's nothing medically wrong with her; there's nothing more they can do. They said I should put her in a facility; twenty-four-hour care. I couldn't do that to her, Lena. I just couldn't."

"No."

The little girl in the bed resembled Reyanne, a slightly older version, with hair a shade more honey where Rey's was flaxen. Lena's heart caught in her chest, this child shared blood with her baby. It was the closest thing to her, so she couldn't help herself when she approached the bed, bent low, and swept her black hair back to press her lips to the child's cool forehead, breathing in deeply the scent of a child. The hard knot in her chest began to loosen for the first time in nearly a year.

"When did you say the accident was, Paul?"

"February 21st."

She looked back at him in disbelief.

"Reyanne died on February 21st."

Lena didn't believe in coincidence, but what on earth could it mean, and why? Paul was stunned as well; was it fortune or fate, or just life's cruel sense of humor at the expense or mortals that would twist their lives so? He watched the still beautiful, familiar stranger with his daughter from the doorway, unable to look away.

Despite what Lena likely thought, Paul had felt an emotion that could've been love towards Lena all those years ago, had it a chance to grow. But he had an obligation to his family and loved them, as well. They needed him more than the headstrong beauty ever could. He'd handled everything wrong, and life had made him pay dearly. He lost *everything*; first his lovely Lena, then his wife and daughter, and Luke was as far as he could get on the other side of the country. Then there was the daughter he never knew.

He had no right to grieve the child but grieve he did. For all that was lost and forever more impossible, for never seeing her face and giving her the love she so deserved, for leaving Lena to fend for herself, for them both alone in the world. *What kind of man am I*, he thought in disgust.

As if reading his thoughts, Lena walked purposefully to the lost man in the doorway and took his rough hand in her soft one and said with a sad sigh,

"You're just human, Paul. You've paid enough. I don't have it in me to be angry anymore, okay? You got a sick little girl there, and she needs you."

"I know, I know Lena. But I- she can't hear me. I— I don't know what to do."

"Well, you just get over there and love her, Paul. That's what you do. You tell her to get her ass back home to her papa. You beg her. I don't know, you *will* her back to you. My girl is gone, I can't..." her voice broke, "I can't get my girl back. But you can. You can get your girl back, I know it. She needs you to bring her back. You need it, too."

For the first time since the accident, the heavy weight lifted off Paul's weary shoulders. Lena was right, of course. Together they approached the bed. He looked to Lena for reassurance; she gave him an encouraging nod and placed his hand over his daughter's hand.

"Hey, kiddo. It—it's you papa here. You uh," emotion choked his words. With a shuddered breath, he tried again. "It's time to come back, baby girl. It's time to start living again. Your old man is pretty lonely here, ya know..."

Frustrated, he turned to Lena, "It's not going to work, damn it. I can't—"

"Hi, Papa. Don't cry."

The wan girl in the bed turned her head to Lena next and said,

"Reyanne told me to tell you 'hey.' Oh, and she likes the spire just as much as you thought she would."

13 STRANGER THAN FICTION

Lena stumbled backward and sat down hard in the nurse's vacated chair, her hand to her open mouth. Tears sprang from her disbelieving eyes and a sound like a moan, and a gasp escaped her lips. The agony and joy of this incredible but true message from her baby… there were no adequate words she could find.

"Hey, sweetheart. You, uh, you saw-" he gulped hard against the knot in his throat, "you saw Reyanne?"

"Yes, Papa. We had a lot of time to get to know each other."

Lena, listening from the chair, regained some of her composure and asked, "You...you were with Reyanne?"

"Yes, ma'am, I was. I told her to stop biting her nails, but she wouldn't."

Paul and Lena both chuckled, despite their shock.

"We went exploring in the woods and, oh! I met your folks, too. Teddy and Idina? Teddy is a practical joker, and your mama is nice as can be. There's also Tommy and Megan, and an Irish Setter named Sunshine! Papa, can we get a dog like that, too?"

Confused and amused, Paul stammered, I-uh, sure thing, sweetheart." To Lena, he said, "It's- it's impossible, isn't it? I mean, how..."

Lena returned his bewildered stare and shrugged. Then, to Shayne,

"Shayne, honey? Is- is Reyanne here now? In this room with us?"

Shayne's brows furrowed as she looked around the room and through the doorway, then she shook her head sadly.

"I can't see her anymore. I'm real sorry. If it helps at all, I do believe she's here, even if we can't see or hear her."

"Oh, little girl, it helps more than you could ever know. Thank you. Thank you from the bottom of my heart. You gave me something I thought was gone, but now I know, I understand. For the first time in a while, I feel like I might just be okay again, all thanks to you."

It was true, Lena felt a lightness in her heart and mind that she hadn't known since running away from the old Victorian house across the street. Just then, the night nurse returned. She let out a surprised gasp at the sight of the woken girl, then clapped her hands in delight. Her joy was genuine and burnt through some of the shocked haze Paul and Lena were in. The three adults laughed and hugged each other as Shayne watched them with a smile.

"Young lady," said the nurse, becoming business-like all at once, "I am Nurse Johanna, and it is lovely to see those beautiful eyes! How are you feeling, my dear?"

Johanna bustled about the room, grabbing a stethoscope and shooing Paul and Lena aside so she could tend to her patient. After a few moments, she seemed satisfied and turned to the two adults.

"It would appear as though my work here is finished. If you don't mind, I'll stay through till dawn, then I'll be on my way. Shayne will need some follow up care with her primary doctor, and then I expect all she'll be needing is fresh air, good food and time. However, for a child who hasn't opened her eyes or spoken a word in eight months, she is doing remarkably well."

"All thanks to you and her day nurse. I—I've been useless…"

"Now, none of that! Your little girl is going to be right as rain, and so are you. All of you. Now, tomorrow is a new day, and you two look exhausted."

She was right, of course, but Paul was afraid to leave Shayne's side for fear of her slipping away again.

"Papa? Miss Lena? It's alright; I promise I'm not going anywhere again. And I won't forget about Reyanne, either. Nurse is right, we're going to be okay."

They couldn't help but smile through their tears at the child consoling the adults. They each kissed her forehead, and with a whispered 'thank you' to Johanna, they quietly left the room. The nurse smiled and motioned for them to go on and settled back in her chair for the rest of the predawn day.

They walked down the stairs, but rather than going to the kitchen, Paul led Lena to the front porch, pausing only to grab a thick blanket from the chest by the door. He guided a willing Lena to the old porch swing and wrapped the blanket around them before sitting down. Together, they watched the sun rise onto a new day, a new life in peaceful silence, their heads together and their warm breath misting in the cool air.

14 THE FINDER OF LOST
SOULS

It was strange to see her mother in the arms of a man, the arms of *her father* no less, but Reyanne smiled at the unlikely pair on the porch swing. The hardness in Lena's face had smoothed away; she was truly beautiful, her mother. She studied her father, too.

She thought perhaps she had his nose and the same shaped eyes. Reyanne got closer to the man she'd have called daddy. Or maybe 'papa' as Shayne did? She smelled his scent; like soap and cotton and something she didn't recognize, but it was nice.

She thought, *I like him*. His face was square; his chin and cheeks stubbled with grey and sandy brown hair. She suddenly wanted to feel the prickly hairs and trace his strong jaw, so she tentatively reached out her small hand and gently touched his face. She could feel the bristle; it was softer than she'd expected. Slowly, he lifted his own hand and, just as gently as she, placed it over hers. She gasped at the surprise. *He can feel me!*

Carefully, as one would move when sighting a deer in the woods, Paul turned his head. He kept his hand over hers, warm on his cheek, and gazed into his daughter's wide blue eyes. He didn't speak, he barely breathed. One tear welled and then rolled from his eye and slipped through their fingers. They stayed like that as the sun slowly rose red in the sky. As it did, Reyanne began to fade. When the sun crested, Paul blinked, and she was gone. His hand, still on his cheek, recalled the warmth of hers for a few moments longer.

15 REDEMPTION

The days and weeks that followed were strange and wonderful... and hard. In a way, for Lena, it was like losing her daughter all over again. Only this time, the loss wasn't felt alone, *she* was not alone. She and Shayne had begun to develop a special relationship, not like mother and daughter, but close. Together, they decided that they would have to just accept the strange, inexplicable gift they'd been given. They were finding peace from their pain at last.

Lena's newfound peace led her to soften her plans for poor Travis Angel, and though she made it clear that they would never be together, he was welcome to stay in the old Victorian for as long as he wished. His heartache was tempered by his relief and genuine happiness for Lena's sudden calm. All he wanted was for her to be happy, after all.

As for her feelings towards Paul, and his for her, they were tentative as well. They decided to start with friendship because truly they were strangers with a history that didn't fit into their present. Neither knew whether it could or would ever be more, but they did know they had Shayne's ardent approval.

And as for Shayne; her road to recovery was not easy, but she knew it *would* get easier. She had faith. She also had a family again, even if it was unconventional. She kept her promise to Lena and told her everything she remembered about her time spent with Reyanne. Together they laughed and cried; she even brought Lena to the clearing where they both swore they could feel *something*. Whatever it was, it brought them peace and comfort. Paul built them a bench from a fallen log, and they planted flowers.

In the spring, Paul surprised Shayne with an Irish Setter puppy; it was a descendant of Sunshine, with earned her the moniker Sunshine Too.

Suddenly, Shayne remembered…

"But papa, what about your allergies?"

"Your old man is going to get shots, but you still have to keep that mutt clean and off the furniture! Got it?"

"Got it!"

Paul caught Lena's eye and winked. She laughed, shaking her head at his indulgence but feeling pleased as well. The foursome walked into the woods, man and woman arm and arm, bouncing child and barking dog leading the way.

The lost souls had found peace and redemption at last. They were alright.

A NOTE FROM THE AUTHOR

Thank you for reading the story of the Lost and Found Girls. I hope you've enjoyed it as much as I enjoyed bringing these characters to life! If so, I'd be grateful if you'd leave a review on either Boobbub, Amazon, or Goodreads. I love hearing from readers at authorelsakurt@gmail.com, too! Xo, Elsa

To Leave a review on Goodreads:

https://www.goodreads.com/author/show/15177316.Elsa_Kurt

For Bookbub:

https://www.bookbub.com/authors/elsa-kurt

And for Amazon:

https://amazon.com/author/elsakurt

ABOUT THE AUTHOR

Elsa Kurt is a multi-genre, indie & traditionally published author, brand designer, life coach, and motivational speaker. She currently has six novels independently published, as well as three novellas published with Crave Publishing in their Craving: Country, Craving: Loyalty, and Craving: Billions anthologies. She is a lifelong New England resident and married mother of two grown daughters. When not writing, designing, or talking her head off, she can be found gardening, hiking, kayaking, and just about anywhere outdoors. Or, you could just find Elsa on social media:

https://facebook.com/authorelsakurt/
https://instagram.com/authorelsakurt/
https://twitter.com/authorelsakurt
https://www.goodreads.com/author/show/15177316.
Elsa_Kurt

https://allauthor.com/profile/elsakurt/
https://amazon.com/author/elsakurt
and her website, http://www.elsakurt.com

EXCERPT FROM PREQUEL TO

LOST AND FOUND GIRLS...

FINDERS KEEPERS

1 DUMBSTRUCK

The moment Paul Steward saw Sarah Anne Prescot, he was dumbstruck. Thursday, September ninth. Intro to American Literature, Ashwin Tullis University, three minutes past nine a.m. *That's* the moment he saw the love of his life for the first time. She strode into the classroom, short heels clicking on the linoleum, long, honey-blonde ponytail swinging, her small chin thrust out and her back straight.

It wasn't just Paul's eyes on her. Everyone looked up—as people do when someone new walks into a quiet room—and he doubted many of the men's eyes returned to their papers. Not that he could peel his eyes from her long enough to be certain. She handed Professor Schultz a slip of paper and murmured what was likely an apology for entering the class late. Then—perhaps sensing the many eyes upon her— turned her head slowly, letting her cool gaze sweep over the room. They paused at Paul.

Did she give the smallest of nods, the tiniest of smiles? It happened so quickly, her green eyes—yes, he could see they were a shade of green that reminded him of Florida springs—flicked away from his brown ones so smoothly that he could argue against his notion. The professor motioned her to the only available seat, in was in Paul's row toward the back. She would have to walk by him. She looked straight ahead as she passed, leaving in her wake a fresh, citrusy scent. His skin prickled as if electrically charged.

Paul couldn't recall one thing that was taught in Intro to American Lit on Thursday, September ninth, but he could recall with ease the exact shade of blue on Sarah's boat-neck blouse—it was navy—and the way the points of her collarbone peeked out. He could describe the pattern of freckles across the bridge of her nose as if it were the constellation and draw the curve of her jawline as if he'd traced it a million times with his fingertips. He needed to speak to her, to hear what her voice sounded like. After class. He would approach her after class, before anyone else could get the chance.

The moment class dismissed, Paul jumped from his seat with such abruptness that the girl beside him yelped. He put his hand on her shoulder and apologized. She flushed crimson and batted her eyes at Paul, but he's already forgotten her and moved toward the back of the row. The chair that had held the honey-haired, citrus sweet woman of his dreams was empty, but the purse that had been slung over her narrow shoulder hung from the backrest. He looked to the doorway, catching sight of the swish of ponytail before she was swallowed by the crowd of college students passing between classes.

He grabbed it from the chair, scooped up his books from his desk and hurried to the door. Perhaps he could catch her before she—

"Oh!"

"Sorry, sorry. Are you alright," Paul stammered. It was her. He found himself looking down into wide green eyes.

"Are you trying to steal my purse?" A delicate, perfect eyebrow rose over her left eye and a smirk hovered on her pouty pink lips as she craned her neck to look into his eyes.

"I-no. You left your—"

"Well, I'm glad we agree it's my purse," She plucked it from Paul's hands. "Thank you. See you around."

Just like that, she was gone again. Paul watched her disappear, his mouth agape, his hands still gripping an invisible purse. He'd blown it. Now he'd have to go the whole weekend either waiting to see her in class or trying to find her on campus.

"So, let me get this straight," said Dean, Paul's roommate and best friend, "the girl—and I quote— 'of your dreams' walks into your class and you—Paul 'The Man' Stewart—freeze? I'm speechless, bud. Well, I wouldn't worry about it. She'll be like the rest of 'em, falling all over you and fighting each other to get to you."

"First, shut up with that nonsense. Second, if that were a thing—and it's not—she isn't like other girls. She's so…"

"Fine?" Hot? Smokin'?"

"Classy. I was going to go with classy. But, yeah, she's all of those, too."

"Okay, so, since when are you unable to talk to a chick?"

Paul would never say it—he was modest *and* unassuming—but it was true. Getting dates had never been a problem for him. On a list of attractive attributes, all boxes could be checked. Tall: Check. Dark-haired: Check. Handsome: Check. Add to that, perfect teeth, square chin, broad chest, athletic build, and smart. Despite all this, he affected no airs, walked with not a modicum of arrogance, nor did he take advantage of the very willing young women who put themselves in his path.

"I-she didn't give me a chance. She just snatched her purse back and disappeared." Paul dropped down onto the worn leather couch and tossed a tennis ball against the brink face wall inside their apartment living room. "You think she has a boyfriend? She probably does, right? A girl like that, she definitely has a boyfriend. Probably a fiancé, even.

Dean stood in the kitchen doorway, a cold beer poised before his mouth. He lowered it, shaking his head, "Listen to you, man. Next, you're gonna start saying things like, 'love at first sight' and drawing hearts on your notebook. Come to the party tonight. Maybe your dream girl will be there."

Paul did go to the party. He spent the whole night looking for the girl, asked everyone and anyone if they knew her, and left without Dean long before the drunken bash ended. The next day, Friday, Paul had only two classes. He spent the time in between searching in vain for the girl whose name he didn't even know. Library, campus café, bookstore, along the narrow cobblestoned street in town where the university students and towns folk shopped. He wandered through the corner market, and into the package store, then out to the sprawling park in the center of town. He walked around the man-made pond and stole surreptitious glances and the couples on blankets and women on benches. At last, her returned to the apartment, disappointed and feeling foolish.

When Monday morning finally rolled around, he revived. He knew he'd see her in class again, affording him another chance at asking her out. He burst through the classroom door ten minutes early, startling Professor Schultz who was at the board writing out a long question regarding John Updike's depiction of Harry 'Rabbit' Angstrom's personal angst.

"Slow down, Mr. Stewart. Class does not begin for another ten minutes," admonished the professor before returning his attention to the board.

Paul looked around the empty room, at her empty seat and his shoulders dropped. He'd build a scenario in his head—they'd both arrive early to class, laugh at their mutual punctuality, then fall into easy conversation, which would lead to coffee after class, then—

"Mr. Steward? You're blocking the doorway. Kindly take your seat if you plan on staying."

Paul finally noticed the back up of students behind him, muttered an apology and took his seat. Class began with no sign of *her*. He glanced repeatedly at the clock above the door, mentally ticking off the minutes as they passed. At six minutes past nine, she–the honey-gold haired goddess—breezed in. She gave no apology, said not a word, and strolled to her seat. Professor Schultz said nothing. He merely lowered his reading glasses as he watched her sashay into her seat. Once situated, she nodded regally at him, as if permitting him to continue. He cleared his throat and obliged. Paul snuck a glance back at her under the guise of asking the classmate behind him a question. She caught him, her eyebrow flicked up, her lips softened briefly, then she averted her eyes. He was assessed and dismissed in seconds.

As he'd done on Thursday, Paul sprang from his chair with the intention of catching her before she left, but the girl he'd startled last week had an agenda of her own and grabbed his arm.

"Hey, I'm having a really hard time with Updike. You think maybe we could get together tonight and go over our notes? We could, um, use my dorm room. My roommate is going to be at her boyfriend's, so—"

"Ah, thanks, but I have plans already. Another time, maybe?" He tried to pull away, but she tightened her grip.

"Tomorrow night, then?"

"Tomorrow? Oh, uh, I—listen, I've got to go. I'll catch up with you." He turned away, toward the back of the room, but it was too late, she was gone again. He pushed and side-stepped his way from the room and out onto the campus courtyard and shielded his eyes from the still-warm September sun. His eyes scanned the heads and faces all around him for sight of her ponytail, her sardonic, knowing expression, or even the pale-yellow blouse she'd worn that day. It was to no avail; he'd lost her again.

Dejected, he sought out a free bench on the green and plopped down heavily. He had an hour before his Psychology class and needed to review his notes. And try to keep his mind off her.

"Aren't you my purse thief?" A shadow fell over his notebook.

Paul looked up just as she tilted her head to the side, allowing the sun to blind him. He squinted and shielded his eyes with his palm.

"Thief? No, more like good Samaritan. I was going to bring it to you, but—"

"Hmm. Likely story. The least you could do is take me out for a drink. By was of penance, that is."

"Penance, huh? Okay, how about tonight?"

"Tonight? Are you under the impression that I'd just make myself free at the drop of your hat, Mr. Stewart? You'll have to do better than that. Try again."

"No, I-you," Paul took a deep breath and tried again. "Would you like to go out sometime for a drink?"

"Sometime? Well, *that's* awfully vague. Makes a girl think you don't really want to ask her out. Paul Stewart, I was told you were quite the ladies' man. I am beginning to have my doubts. Tell me, do you even know my name?"

"Um, no, I—" Paul was at a disadvantage in every way. She knew his name, was standing over him, and had him tongue-tied. He stood and tried again, this time looking down at her. "I apologize. May I ask your name? Please?"

"You may. I'm Sarah Anne Prescot. How do you do?" She extended her hand and gazed at Paul expectantly.

A slow, goofy smile spread across his face and he took her small hand in his large one. "Hello, Sarah Anne Prescot. I'm Paul Stewart and I'm doing much better now, thank you. May I take you out for dinner tomorrow night?"

"Oh, skipping right over drinks and going straight to dinner, are we? What if we have nothing to say to each other?" Her hand was still in his.

"What if we talk all night?"

"What if we can't stand each other?"

"What if we can't stand to be apart from each other?"

"Well, you have an answer for everything, don't you? May I have my hand back please?" Paul let go reluctantly. "Thank you. Pick me up at seven p.m., Waller Terrace. Don't be late." She turned on her heel and walked away without a backward glance.

Paul watched her until she disappeared around a corner, half expecting her to meet up with a group of giggling girlfriends, but there were none in sight. Something—a little voice in his head, perhaps—told him Sarah Anne Prescot was trouble with a capital T, but he found himself not caring one bit.

OTHER WORKS BY ELSA KURT

LIVVY TAKES THE LONG WAY- (Contemporary fiction) One woman's journey through marriage and divorce & starting over.

The Awkward Woman's Guide to Dating (After Divorce)- (Contemporary Fiction) A humorous look at life after divorce.

STILL HERE (Contemporary Fiction)- A beautiful, unforgettable love story with a twist.

The Writer's Romance: Hallmark style sweet romantic comedy.

Mae's Café: Book One in Welcome to Chance, a small-town series.

Rosabelle's Way: Book Two in Welcome to Chance Available 7/2019

Georgie's Secret: Book Three in Welcome to Chance Available 9/2019

Billionaire's Club: A Billion Reason

Craving Country: Tomorrow Always Comes

Craving: Loyalty: The Devil's Own

<u>You Wrote It, Now What?</u> A guide for aspiring writers.